THE FAITHFUL SIREN

MERRY FARMER

THE FAITHFUL SIREN

Copyright ©2019 by Merry Farmer

Cover design by Erin Dameron-Hill (the miracle-worker)

ASIN: B07ZG3MPV8

Paperback ISBN: 9781704216676

Click here for a complete list of other works by Merry Farmer.

If you'd like to be the first to learn about when the next books in the series come out and more, please sign up for my newsletter here: http://eepurl.com/RQ-KX

 Created with Vellum

For Jess and Mike

Yay! At last!

CHAPTER 1

LONDON – AUTUMN, 1816

"This is a tragedy. An utter tragedy of Shakespearian proportions."

Lady Imogen Marlowe stared at her image in the long mirror propped in a corner of her bedroom, miserable to her core. Too much of her life had been misery, ever since her mother's death nearly a decade ago. But things had gone from bad to worse at the summer house party hosted by Lord Rufus and Lady Caroline Herrington in Shropshire six weeks before.

"At least you look beautiful," Imogen's sister, Alice, said, coming to stand beside her. "I am shocked that Father allowed you to buy a new gown for the ball tonight."

Imogen's heart sank further. "Father didn't buy it for

1

me, Lord Cunningham did." She spoke as though Lord Cunningham had purchased the ax that would lop off her head soon.

Alice slipped a supportive arm around Imogen's waist and the two of them stood there in silence, regarding their gloomy reflections. Their fates had been sealed at the Herrington house party. Their father had managed the coup he'd been talking about for years. He'd engaged all three of his daughters to men of title and wealth, or at least reputation and wealth, in the case of their eldest sister, Lettuce. Poor Lettuce had been all but abducted by the odious Mr. Pigge—a merchant with grand plans and disgusting character—who had already forcibly married Lettuce and carried her off on a ship bound for America.

Imogen's and Alice's fates were no less horrific. Alice was betrothed to the Aegirian Count Fabian Camoni—who had abandoned her almost as soon as the engagement was final, promising to come for her at Christmas. Alice was lucky to have the reprieve. Imogen, on the other hand, wasn't so fortunate. Her father had shackled her to Lord Cunningham—a lascivious bounder who was as old as her father and who had made no secret about the reasons he wanted Imogen. She was fated to spend her marriage on her back, being used in ways she shuddered to imagine, until she was too worn out for the purpose. And then who knew what would become of her?

"Come on," Alice said at last, shaking herself and drawing Imogen away from the mirror. "This is practically your first outing since returning to London after the house party. You should enjoy it."

Imogen sighed and walked with Alice to her bed. The sisters sat together, shoulders drooping. "It won't be the same without you," she swallowed, "or Letty."

"I know," Alice hugged her from the side, leaning her head against Imogen's shoulder. "Father is beyond cruel for locking us in the house and forbidding us to go out."

"I never would have been so happy to attend Lady Malvis and Lord Ainsley's wedding if we'd had any other opportunity to so much as go outside and take a walk," Imogen added.

Alice snorted with surprised laughter. "That was an event, wasn't it?"

Imogen cracked a weak smile as well. The one and only time she and Alice had been let out of the house in the past six weeks was to attend the wedding. Lady Malvis was Lord Cunningham's daughter, so of course his fiancée was required to attend the ceremony and wedding breakfast afterward. And Alice was right, it was an event. Lord Ainsley was the most eccentric man she'd ever known. He'd insisted that he and Lady Malvis should wear matching outfits of lavender and puce and that the flowers should follow the same color scheme. He'd doted ridiculously on Lady Malvis and recited sugary poetry to her several times throughout the day. As soon as the wedding was over, they'd departed for America on the same ship as Lettuce and Mr. Pigge—neither of whom attended the wedding.

More than the silliness of the wedding, Imogen was grateful that Lady Malvis's big day meant that Lord Cunningham had been forced to delay his own marriage until a suitable amount of time after his daughter's wedding. Imogen had had a reprieve, but that was now over.

And there was one other element to the whole farce, one giant, painful twist that made a rotten situation even more disastrous.

Alice glanced mournfully at Imogen and asked, "Have you...have you heard from Thaddeus at all?" in a quiet voice.

Imogen heaved a sigh and shook her head, her tears flowing at last. "No," she admitted with a wet sniffle, not even trying to brush away her tears. "But I'm certain it's not because he hasn't tried to contact me." She squared her shoulders and attempted to be strong as she went on. "Lord Thaddeus Herrington is the most wonderful man on the planet. He is dashing and brave and so handsome. The way he kissed me at the house party and the way he promised to care for me always was glorious and heartfelt."

"But you haven't had so much as a letter smuggled in by the servants since then?" Alice's voice went even quieter.

Imogen dropped her shoulders. "No," she moaned. "But I don't believe for a moment that it is Thaddeus's fault. Father must be preventing him from contacting me. Father and Lord Cunningham."

"It makes sense that they would," Alice sighed. "You would run off with Lord Herrington at the drop of a hat if you had a chance to."

It wasn't a question. Alice knew full well that Imogen had given her whole heart to Thaddeus at the house party. He was everything Lord Cunningham was not and then some. He was young—too young, some might say. As the youngest son of an earl, he wasn't much better than a middle-class tradesman, but Thaddeus had ideas and he had ambition. He'd spoken to Imogen about his plans to defy convention and go into trade. He'd gone on and on with rhapsodic elegance about the opportunities open to young men of insight and boldness, thanks to the mechanization of industry and the vast increase in sea trade. He'd painted such a beautiful picture of the future the two of them could have, if Imogen was bold enough to escape her father's and Lord Cunningham's clutches.

But since they were heartlessly torn apart at the end of the house party, since Imogen had been locked away in her father's house, as though it were a prison, she'd had no contact with Thaddeus at all.

"He will find a way to reach you," Alice reassured her with a hug. "He loves you, and doesn't our book say that love conquers all?"

Alice leapt off the bed and crossed to the bureau to retrieve part of a broken book. She carried the book back to Imogen, thrusting it into her hands.

Imogen smoothed her hands over the already worn pages of the book as though it were an old friend. "*The*

Secrets of Love," she sighed the title of the book. "Wouldn't it be grand if these pages contained exactly the sort of secret that could save us?"

"Perhaps they do," Alice said, a faint note of hope in her voice. "That is to say, look right there."

She pointed to the heading on the page Imogen had opened to: Daring to Love. Imogen stared at the words, wondering if she had it within her to dare at all anymore.

"Here," Alice said, taking the book from her. "I'll read it aloud to cheer you up." She cleared her throat. "Love can seem unattainable to those who live in a cruel world, but that should not prevent you from dreaming of amazing possibilities. Anything is possible with love. Even the shepherdess can dream of marrying the prince and make it possible if she is willing to embrace boldness. She will find that the man she loves becomes the prince in her eyes and in her heart."

Imogen huffed a defeated laugh. "The author of The Secrets of Love must not have been part of our London society. If she were, she would know that we must be resigned to our fates."

"But are you?" Alice asked. "Are you truly resigned to the fate of marrying Lord Cunningham? Do you hold out no hope that Lord Herrington will rescue you in the end?"

Imogen bit her lip, gently taking her section of the book from Alice's hands. "No, I am not truly resigned," she whispered. She was certain that hope filled her eyes as she went on with, "I know Thaddeus. Even though he has been unable to contact me since Shropshire, I know that he is thinking about me and I know he is looking for ways to take me away from all this."

"Then you must remain faithful to him in your heart," Alice insisted. "You must believe in him."

"I do. I most certainly do. But—"

Imogen was interrupted by a soft knock on the door. A moment later, one of the maids opened it and said with a look of pure regret, "Lady Imogen, your father and Lord Cunningham are waiting downstairs."

Imogen exchanged a look with Alice, then stood. She walked her section of the book back to her bureau, put it down as reluctantly as could be, then headed for the door.

"Pray for me, dear sister," she said as she reached the door. "And pray for Thaddeus to find a way to reach me."

"I will," Alice vowed. "You know I will."

Part of Imogen wished that Alice could accompany her downstairs to face Lord Cunningham, but in truth, she didn't wish the awkwardness of being in Lord Cunningham's presence on anyone. And sadly, Lord Cunningham did not disappoint.

"Ah, my sweet. You look every bit as delicious as I knew you would be in that gown," the horrible man said, eyeing Imogen up and down as she reached the bottom of the stairs, where Lord Cunningham and her father were waiting.

Imogen glanced down at her dress, feeling far more self-conscious than she had regarding herself in the mirror. The gown had been made in a style that would raise the eyebrows of even the most daring members of the *ton*. The bodice was cut so low that the tops of her nipples were in danger of peeking out if she moved too suddenly. The box in which the gown had been delivered contained no fichu to protect her modesty either. An alarming expanse of her breasts was visible for anyone to see. The gown was made of the thinnest of muslins as well. Imogen had the sinking feeling that if she stood in the wrong sort of light, her entire form would be visible.

Lord Cunningham seemed to confirm her suspicions as he edged his way around her, backing her toward one of the lamps. "Yes," he said, rubbing a hand over his mouth. "I think you will do quite nicely." He underscored his statement by blatantly reaching for his breeches to adjust the growing bulge there.

Imogen lowered her head, feeling as dirty as if he'd stood her on a dais in a public square and stripped her naked for a crowd of men to look at. Her insides shriveled at the thought that this would be her future if Thaddeus was unable to reach her. She'd heard rumors about how men like Lord Cunningham shared their wives with their friends once they grew tired of them. The very thought was enough to bring her to tears again.

"Shut up," her father snapped, even though she didn't say anything. "You're going to a ball. Young ladies adore going to balls. Lord Cunningham is going to announce the time of your wedding this Friday. I will be triumphant at last. So stop your sniveling."

"Yes, Father," Imogen managed to squeak, though she couldn't stop the tears from falling. Where was Thaddeus and when would he finally come to rescue her?

AT LAST, THE MOMENT HAD COME. THADDEUS adjusted the jacket of the footman's livery he'd donned in order to infiltrate Lord Mapplethorpe's ball and fell in line with the other extra footmen that had been hired for the evening.

"I still can't believe you want to do this, my lord," Oliver, the legitimate footman who had slipped him into the ranks of the hired help for the evening said as they collected trays of cakes and tarts to take up to the refreshment room. "A nobleman masquerading as a footman?"

Thaddeus sent the young man a mischievous grin. "I'm barely a nobleman," he said, taking one of the trays. "And I'm doing it for a good cause."

"What cause would that be, my lord?" the man asked as they carried their trays along the busy downstairs hall to the servants' stairs.

"Best not to call me that where anyone might overhear," Thaddeus whispered as they started up."

"Sorry, my—um, sir." Oliver's face went bright red with embarrassment.

"It's nothing," Thaddeus went on. "I'm here because it's the only chance I've had in weeks to see the woman I love."

They reached a bend in the stairs and Oliver turned

to Thaddeus, his brow lifting in surprise. "The woman you love? How does a toff like you—begging your pardon —not get to see the woman he loves, or any other woman for that matter?"

"Her father is an ogre," Thaddeus explained, deep hatred for Lord Marlowe welling within him. "And he's shackled her to an even worse ogre."

"Your lady is married, then?" Oliver looked uncertain.

"Not if I can help it," Thaddeus said, bristling with determination. "The marriage hasn't happened yet. Her father's kept her locked up tight. Everything I've tried to get word to her has failed, so here we are."

"Playing the part of a footman at a ball so's you can speak to her?" Oliver asked. He shook his head. "I wouldn't believe it if I hadn't seen it with my own eyes."

"Love makes us do strange things," Thaddeus agreed with a humorless laugh.

"That it does, my—um, sir."

Their conversation ended as they passed through the doorway that separated the world of the servants from the world of their masters. It had always amazed Thaddeus that the two worlds could exist side-by-side with barely any interaction. He was ashamed to say that he hardly knew anything about the lives of the men and women who had served him and his family for years. But in the painful weeks since his brother and sister-in-law's house party, his entire attitude about the world had changed.

If there was one thing that Thaddeus's father—and

even his brother, Rufus—criticized him the most for, it was being young and complacent, taking things for granted. As little as six weeks ago, he would have argued that he wasn't taking anything for granted at all. He knew he wouldn't inherit the sort of wealth and title his brother was in line for. Their father might have been an earl, but their family was newer than some and didn't have the historical roots that much of the aristocracy had. He would have to make a life for himself and he'd known that for years. That was what had led to his interest in business and the growing industries that were transforming the country from a rural idyll to a modern, mechanical marvel. He had wanted to find a way to capitalize on that for years, though his father considered his interest in business scandalously beneath his class.

What Thaddeus had taken for granted for so long was the idea that he would be able to marry whomever he wanted whenever he wanted and that there would be no impediments to their union. He'd fallen in love with Lady Imogen Marlowe at first sight. They had slipped off to spend more than a little time together during his brother's scandalous house party. But then Lord Marlowe had announced Imogen was to marry the horrific Lord Cunningham.

Well, Thaddeus wouldn't have it. And that evening, he intended to do something about it.

"This way, um, sir," Oliver murmured, drawing Thaddeus with him into the large refreshment room set up near the heart of the house and the ball. "You can set those things down on that table." Oliver nodded to a table to one side of the room.

Lord Mapplethorpe had gone to great expense to have the treats for his party made by the famous confectioner, Mr. Jonathan Foster. The tables looked like something out of a fairy story the way they were laden with cakes that looked like flowers and mushrooms. An entire tray of sweets had been designed to look like small woodland creatures, which was magnificent...until a particularly rotund and red-faced lord bit the head off a small squirrel and laughed uproariously. Mr. Foster was there himself, along with his wife, Sophie—who was, perhaps fortunately, fully-clothed and not covered with sugar for this particular event. Thaddeus had attended a party in the spring where Mrs. Foster was the centerpiece of the refreshment room wearing nothing but sugar paste. He was embarrassed to remember how he'd "entertained" himself later that night while remembering the sight of her luscious body. That was before he'd met Imogen, though. In the last few weeks, Imogen's image was the one he'd imagined while getting himself off.

Those sorts of thoughts weren't going to help him accomplish his mission, however. He delivered his tray to the proper table, then inched back to the doorway, peering out into the hall. There were any number of men and women who might have recognized him milling about the front hall and making their way into the grand ballroom. Thaddeus was particularly noticeable with his ginger hair. He'd combed a bit of ash through it in an attempt to darken it for the evening, but nothing dampened the power of ginger hair. He had to rely on the fact that no one from the *ton* would expect to see him in footman's livery, dashing about with the servants.

Oliver didn't try to stop him as he slipped out of the room entirely, edging his way down the hall until he could peek into one of the doorways leading to the ballroom. He'd heard word that Mapplethorpe had invited anyone who was anyone to his ball, and so far, that seemed to be the case. The evening was still young, but it promised to be a crush in no time. That could only help, as far as Thaddeus was concerned.

A quick scan of the ballroom proved that Imogen hadn't arrived yet, so he headed back toward the refreshment room.

"Did you find your girl?" Oliver asked as he exited the room.

"Not yet," Thaddeus said. "She might just be—"

No sooner had he started to speculate why Imogen was late, when she walked through the front door, a step behind her father and Lord Cunningham.

"That's her," he whispered to Oliver, turning to stand by the young man's side.

"What, the one with the—" Oliver made the shape of twin orbs over his chest.

"That's the one," Thaddeus whispered.

"No wonder, sir," Oliver said with a sly grin.

Thaddeus would have treated the man to a sharp elbow in the ribs for his comment, but he had to admit that Imogen was dressed like some sort of tart. That could only be Lord Cunningham's doing. The man had made no secret of why he wanted to marry Imogen. He'd been bragging about the things he planned to do with her all over London in the last six weeks. And Imogen looked miserable to be dressed the way she was. Thaddeus was more determined than ever to move heaven and earth to get her out of her current situation.

Those thoughts were bolstered as she glanced up, as if guided by some sort of sixth sense, and looked right at him. Thaddeus stood straighter, smiling at her. Imogen's expression was shocked at first, but then it filled with a sort of joy that made Thaddeus feel as though he could do anything.

He thought fast, pointing down the hall and across a bit, to a closed door that led to one of the parlors the family had deemed off-limits to party guests. A moment later, just as Lord Marlowe and Lord Cunningham came to a stop before entering the ballroom, Imogen nodded to him, understanding in her expression. Even though her father and Lord Cunningham turned to speak to her with frowns, Thaddeus felt as though they'd won an important victory.

"Give my excuses to whoever asks about my absence," he told Oliver before heading as subtly as he could across the hall to the closed parlor.

CHAPTER 2

*I*mogen's heart shot to her throat the moment she noticed Thaddeus lingering at the side of the hall. It had been so long since she'd laid eyes on him that she'd begun to question whether he was just a dream her aching heart had conjured up. But there he was... dressed like a footman?

"Balls are such a nuisance," Lord Cunningham grumbled to her father a few steps ahead. "If I didn't want to court Mapplethorpe's favor, I would have skipped the bloody thing."

"Hear, hear," her father answered. He followed that by snorting in derision at a group of excited young ladies that passed him on their way to the ballroom. "Events like this are just an excuse for men like Mapplethorpe to show off and empty-headed young ladies to trap unsuspecting men into marriage."

Lord Cunningham guffawed in agreement. Imogen

15

watched him and her father closely, until she was absolutely certain neither man had noticed Thaddeus. Then she stole a second glance at her one, true love, her heart overflowing with joy and relief.

Though he was much too far off for anything he might say to be heard, Thaddeus communicated with crystal clarity all the same. He nodded to one of the closed doors down the hall. He wanted her to meet him there. A thrill shot through her. She'd heard more than a few whispered stories of ladies meeting gentlemen in private rooms during balls before. They were the sorts of things that were talked about with reverence and awe, and more than a bit of shock. More than a few reputations had been ruined by such meetings. Imogen didn't care if her reputation was tossed in the mud and trampled on if it meant she could run away with Thaddeus. She nodded back to him, indicating she would meet up with him as soon as she could.

"Imogen. What has gotten into you?" her father snapped, nearly frightening Imogen out of her skin. Her father didn't wait for her answer. "We're proceeding into the ballroom. Don't just stand there like an idiot."

"Yes, Father," she said, skittering into motion and nearly falling over the hem of her gown as she did. Her toe caught on the hem, tugging the entire gown down enough so that one of her nipples popped free of the daring neckline. She gasped and rushed to tuck herself back in, all too aware that Lord Cunningham was watching her with greedy eyes and a ruddy complexion.

"Careful," he said in a rough voice. "We wouldn't want every man here to get a look at what is mine."

As they walked on, Imogen had the sickening feeling that was exactly what Lord Cunningham wanted. He had dressed her inappropriately so that he could show off to his friends. As soon as they entered the ballroom, those friends flocked to them, congratulating Lord Cunningham on his conquest and ogling Imogen's nearly exposed breasts as though they knew they would have their chance with her sometime soon. It was pure torture, but she was able to bear it, knowing that Thaddeus was there, that he was waiting for her. All she had to do was figure out how to break away from her father and Lord Cunningham.

Her chance came suddenly, but Imogen was ready.

"Cunningham, would you allow me to dance with your charming betrothed?" one of the lecherous old men flocking around her asked, addressing his question to Imogen's cleavage.

"What?" Lord Cunningham grunted and shrugged. "You actually want to *dance* with the chit? Well, on your head be it." He laughed, slapping his friend on the back.

Imogen hadn't even been properly introduced to the old man. He didn't seem to want to be introduced to anything but her breasts. So she had no qualms at all of using him for her purposes. She took his offered arm, swayed closer to him when he stepped toward the other couples forming lines for the dance, and rejoiced when he trod on the hem of her gown right on cue.

"Oh, dear," she gasped at the ripping sound that followed. Better still, her nipple popped free of the neckline once more. "Oh dear, oh dear."

She did her best to tuck herself away as discreetly as possible while the old man looked as though he would either have a heart attack or embarrass himself then and there in the ballroom. Luckily for Imogen, her father and Lord Cunningham witnessed the whole thing.

"I must go to the retiring room to repair my hem. And to see if I can do something about this bodice," she told them, eyes downcast. She hoped the expression made her look ashamed instead of bristling with excitement at the idea of meeting Thaddeus again. "Please excuse me."

"Oh, all right," her father sighed, rolling his eyes as though she were a trial.

"Hurry back," Lord Cunningham ordered her.

Imogen nodded to him with as much deference as she could muster, then turned and hurried out of the ballroom. She was well aware of people watching her with pity and disapproval as she fled. Even if her gown was a cruel prank and even if the fashion of the day was daring, the *ton* did not approve of nipples flying out in public. At least, not at respectable balls.

By the time she reached the door Thaddeus had nodded to, she didn't care if her breasts were hanging free. She grasped the door handle, said a quick prayer that her deliverance was at hand, and cracked open the door. She poked her head only into the room at first, to make certain Thaddeus was there and any number of other guests were not.

"Imogen." Thaddeus leapt toward her from the fireplace he'd been staring into while waiting for her. "Thank God."

"Thaddeus." She rushed into the room, shutting the door behind her, and flew into his arms, near tears. He caught her and slanted his mouth over hers, kissing her with all the passion of a man who had been denied for too long. She kissed him back with equal fervor, circling her arms around him and digging her fingertips into his back as though she would never let go. "Oh, Thaddeus, my darling. I've missed you so, so much. I haven't known what to do without you." Each declaration was made between bouts of kissing that left her breathless and dizzy.

"Imogen, my love," he said, swaying back at last so that he could look at her. "I've been so terribly worried about you."

"My father has kept me and Alice virtual prisoners in our house," she said, clutching him tightly so that he wouldn't break from her. She had the feeling that if they separated by too much now, they would be separated forever.

"And Lord Cunningham?" Thaddeus's expression turned murderous. "Has he laid a hand on you?"

Imogen shook her head. "Not really. He has attempted to take liberties by walking too close to me and such. And he purchased this alarming gown for me." She glanced down.

Thaddeus did as well. The thundercloud of his expression shifted momentarily to a grin. "Under other circumstances, I would admit to liking this gown quite a bit."

Of all things, Imogen giggled. It was horrific to have Lord Cunningham and his friends stare at her like she was a piece of meat they wanted to devour, but when Thaddeus did the same thing, it filled her with desire and made her ache in delicious places.

That only drove home how awful her situation was.

"Oh, Thaddeus," she sighed, close to weeping once more. "Please take me away from here. Rescue me. Run away with me. Anything."

"That is exactly what I intend to do," he said, then leaned in to kiss her once more. His lips were like magic against hers. The heat that radiated from him infused her with hope. She would have given herself to him then and there. Her body certainly pulsed as though it were ready to. But Thaddeus broke their kiss. "I have a plan," he said, stepping away enough to take her hand and lead her to one of the sofas placed discreetly in the corner of the room.

"Tell me," she said, still unwilling to let go of him entirely as they sat. "Whatever you want to do, I will do it."

"The plan—" he began, but stopped so that he could pull her into his arms and kiss her once more. His mouth was hungry for hers and his hands spread across her sides. The groan deep in his throat was more than enough to tell Imogen how desperately he wanted her.

At last, he broke their kiss, struggling to catch his breath for a moment, then said, "I still have the money that Saif Khan gave me. It isn't much, but it should get us away from London."

"Good," Imogen said, unable to catch her breath herself. She throbbed in distracting places and her mostly-exposed breasts felt heavy and eager to be touched. "Anything. I'll do anything you want." In more ways than simply running away. She would bare herself for anything Thaddeus wanted to do to her, no matter how wicked.

Thaddeus hummed deep in his throat, as though he knew exactly what she meant. He closed a hand over her breast, squeezing gently. His fingers reached for the neckline of her bodice, but he held himself back.

"My father has forbidden me from interfering with you," he said, his voice hoarse with lust. "He has threatened to disown me if I prevent you from marrying Lord Cunningham and attempt to marry you myself."

"And do you care what he says?" she asked, a pinch of trepidation gnawing at her gut.

"Not at all," Thaddeus said with a rush of breath, surging into her for another kiss.

His lips on hers were demanding. His tongue invaded her, thrusting in imitation of even more stunning acts of love. His hand closed more tightly around her breast, and it was all she could do to keep herself from straddling him, opening the falls of his breeches, and riding him like a strumpet.

But they had not secreted themselves in the quiet parlor for an assignation. There were important matters that needed to be dealt with.

"I don't care about money," she panted, barely able to form the words, so desperate was her need for him. "I'd live a pauper's life with you, if that's what it takes for us to be together."

"It won't come to that," he promised, brushing his fingertips along her neckline and over the tops of her breasts. "Aside from Mr. Khan's money, I have skills and ambitions. We may not live an aristocratic life, but we will be comfortable, I swear it."

"And the school," Imogen somehow managed to say as he leaned into her and laid a series of kisses across her neck and shoulder. "The school is always willing to help us."

He paused in his delicious ministrations to glance up at her. "The school?"

"Your sister-in-law, Lady Caro's, school," she reminded him.

He laughed. "I have a hard time remembering any other woman, or anything else at all, when I am with you," he said, following his words with another kiss that had Imogen's sex flaring with heat and moisture. "But you are right. They will help us. In fact, I suspect that all we need to do is get there and we will be home free."

"Then how do we get there?" she asked.

"Like this," he said, lust in his voice and fire in his eyes.

He tipped her to her back, spreading her against the sofa. When her breasts slipped free of her dangerous gown at the gesture, he tugged her bodice down, freeing them entirely. With a mischievous laugh that left her writhing with desire, he bent closer, closing a hand around one of her breasts and holding it so that he could close his mouth over her escaped nipple. She gasped and arched into him as he sucked hard, then swirled his tongue around her tight nipple. The sensations he produced in her were so deep and so heady that she moaned far louder than she should with pleasure.

That only seemed to encourage him. He let go of her breast, reaching for the hem of her skirt instead. In seconds, he'd hitched the flimsy fabric over her hip and pushed her knees apart so that he could stroke the soft, overheated flesh of her inner thigh. She was so primed for pleasure that when his fingers brushed across the opening of her sex, she nearly flew apart.

"God, you're wet," he panted, nuzzling her breasts. "I knew you would be."

"Thinking about you makes me wild," she panted, moving against his hand in search of what she needed from him. "I think about you when pleasuring myself."

He answered her wicked confession with a low hum. Simply touching her didn't seem like enough for him anymore. He thrust two fingers inside of her, causing her to cry out in pleasure. She shuddered as he continued to thrust demandingly, grinding the base of his hand against her clitoris.

"Come for me, my siren," he growled, kissing her breasts and neck.

Imogen was so ready that she burst apart at his command, throbbing and trembling as he brought her to climax. It was pure bliss, absolute pleasure. She gave in to it, wanting to reward him for his faith in her by being every fantasy he had ever had rolled into one. She was his in every way.

As her orgasm began to subside, her thoughts shifted to him. She reached for his breeches, finding him every bit as hard as she knew he would be. With a lazy, sated grin, she slipped off of the sofa and came to rest on her knees between his legs. She fumbled with the fastenings of his breeches, sending him a wicked look, hinting what she was about to do. He didn't try to stop her with flowery platitudes about how she was his angel and shouldn't even think about such things. Instead, when she peeled back his breeches and stroked his hard, hot prick, he arched his hips toward her.

The tip of his cock was already glistening with moisture as she stroked him. The desire that he had just satisfied within her flared to life once more as she wriggled closer to him, then bent forward, drawing him into her mouth. They both groaned as she circled her lips around his head only. She stroked him with her tongue, delighting in the salty, musky taste of him. She teased him for as long as she dared, putting her all into kissing and tormenting him until she was ready. Then she took a deep breath and plunged.

"Christ almighty," he gasped as she took him deep into her mouth. His body tensed and he jerked even deeper into her while clutching the cushions for support. He filled her to the point where her eyes watered and she was in danger of choking, but the pleasured sounds he made and the way he seemed completely at her mercy more than made up for any discomfort.

He was so masculine and so aroused that any shred of good sense or modesty she had went out the window. She gripped his hips hard and bore down on him repeatedly, using her tongue to give him as much sensation as possible. He was large and powerful, and soon his own, jerking movements melded with hers in a heady dance of sensuality. His cries grew more and more desperate and his body tensed until, at last, he pushed her back.

Within a split-second of releasing him, he came with a jet of pearl that shot up between them to a remarkable height. It sullied the hem of his shirt as he grasped himself and worked to a full finish.

"Oh, my," Imogen gasped, clapping a hand to her reddened lips. "I've never seen anything like that."

He laughed and was about to reply when there was a knock at the door. Imogen gasped, as did Thaddeus, but neither of them had time to right themselves or conceal what they'd been up to before the door cracked open and the footman Thaddeus had been speaking to when Imogen had first arrived popped his head in.

"Lady Imogen, you've been missed," the man said quickly. "Your father and Lord Cunningham have begun searching for you. They'll be here in less than a minute." He disappeared as soon as his message was delivered.

Imogen and Thaddeus stood and raced to put themselves to right. It was far easier for Imogen, who merely had to tuck her breasts back into her questionable bodice.

"Go back to your father as quick as you can," Thaddeus ordered as he worked to figure out how to hide the stains that now adorned the front of his shirt and waistcoat. "Can you extend whatever excuse you made to join me here?"

"I told them I needed to go to the retiring room to find a maid to fix my hem," she said, glancing down, distressed that the hem was still torn.

Thaddeus studied her hard for a moment. "You'd do well to run over to the refreshment room as fast as you can. Find a cake with red icing to eat. That could explain your lips and your absence."

Imogen clapped a hand to her mouth, which she realized must be a dead giveaway for what she'd been doing. "I will," she said, turning to rush for the door. She stopped when she reached it and spun back to him. "But what will we do? I cannot return to my father's house. He won't let me out again before my wedding day, and that's only Friday."

Thaddeus frowned and paused in his efforts to clean

up. "I'll think of something. I'll steal you away tonight, I promise. Go back to your father for now. As soon as you see my signal, be ready to run."

"Right. I will."

Imogen nodded, then opened the door and dashed into the hall. She would have given anything to stay with Thaddeus or to run away with him right then and there. But she had faith in his ability to plan and rescue her well and truly by the end of the night. All she had to do in that moment was convince her father and Lord Cunningham that she'd merely gotten lost or failed to keep track of time.

She dashed across the hall to the refreshment room and bolted for the first table that held anything with pink and red icing. Without thinking, she grabbed the first cake and shoved it into her mouth, taking care to smear icing over her mouth.

Thaddeus's plan was a good one, and she executed it just in time.

"Imogen. What are you doing in here?" her father demanded as he and Lord Cunningham marched into the room.

"I beg your pardon?" she asked, her mouth full of cake.

Lord Cunningham's scowl of suspicion faded to his usual, lecherous leer. "I should have known the sweet would be stuffing herself with sweets." He sauntered up to her and wiped a finger over the icing on her lips. He then brought that finger to his mouth and sucked on it. The entire gesture turned Imogen's stomach.

"You stupid girl," her father sighed. "I should have known better than to leave you alone. You came right here instead of finding a maid for that hem, didn't you?" He nodded to her still-ripped hem.

Imogen couldn't bring herself to answer. She merely lowered her head and put the remainder of her emergency cake back on the tray.

"Disgusting," her father hissed, grabbing her arm and yanking her away from the table.

"I don't know," Lord Cunningham said. "There's something about the girl's mischievous feast that makes her look almost debauched." He followed his comment by adjusting his tented breeches as they made their way back across the hall to the ballroom. "I think I can forgive her. This time."

Imogen swallowed hard, praying that neither her father nor Lord Cunningham would pursue the matter further and discover her secret. She glanced around the room as they rejoined the ball, desperate for whatever signal Thaddeus was about to send her when the time came for them to run.

CHAPTER 3

The last thing Thaddeus wanted to do was to leave Imogen to the mercy of her father and Lord Cunningham. He knew they would show no mercy where she was concerned, that they barely thought of her as a person in her own right as well. They saw her as a commodity to be used for their own purposes. He'd seen that sort of treatment happen too many times before to ladies of his acquaintance among the upper classes, and he was through with it.

"Oliver." He caught the arm of his footman friend as the two of them made their way to the end of the hall where the entrance to the servants' stairs stood. "I need your help."

"My help, my lord—I mean, sir?" The young man looked truly baffled by the appeal.

"I need a way to whisk Lady Imogen out of the house and away into the night," Thaddeus went on as the two of them ducked into the busy thoroughfare of the servants' stairs. "Some way that will be discreet but will also enable us to escape to freedom."

Oliver continued to gape at him. "But you're a nob," he said, then shook himself. "That is to say, my lord, you're a better class. Why would you want freedom from all that?"

"Because it's not all it's cracked up to be," Thaddeus answered with a wary grin. "Because having a title comes with a price. I'd rather be a footman permanently if it meant I could live, happy and at peace, with the woman I love."

Oliver answered Thaddeus's speech with a wry look of his own. "Then there's things you don't know about a life in service. If you knew, you'd change your mind. But I'll help you and Lady Imogen escape," he finished before Thaddeus could interrupt him with more arguments about who had the better life. "I've got an idea."

The words were music to Thaddeus's ears. He followed Oliver down the stairs and through a maze of hallways until they reached the kitchen. Lord Mapplethorpe's staff was hard at work, banging pots, chopping vegetables, mixing bowls of batter, and minding a dozen steaming pots and kettles at least. No one seemed to notice two footmen crossing through the chaos to the small door that led out into the mews.

"These mews run the entire length of the block," Oliver explained, walking Thaddeus down to the end so that he could see where they let out. Several carriages were packed into the space, their drivers loitering about, waiting for their masters to be finished with the ball. The lanterns they carried lit the space far more than it would have been on a normal night. That might not be an advantage for the sort of escape Thaddeus had in mind, but it might also be just the thing to put Imogen at ease.

The street outside of the mews was also crowded with carriages and lit with dozens of lanterns, but it was darker, and after a quick glance around, Thaddeus was fairly sure he and Imogen could escape into the night without a problem.

"Good," he said, thumping Oliver on the back as they headed back to the house. "Now I just need to figure out a way to signal for Imogen to come down to the mews."

"Fine ladies don't even know where the mews are, let alone how to get there," Oliver warned him.

Thaddeus stopped just outside Mapplethorpe's kitchen door and turned to Oliver. "Then you'll have to show her the way."

"Me, my lord?" Oliver's brow flew up.

"I cannot do it," Thaddeus said. "Lord Marlowe and Lord Cunningham know me. They might not have picked me out of the crowd upstairs in this livery, but they would know in a trice what was afoot if they saw me directly."

"But how should I convince a fine lady to come with me to a place like this?" Oliver rolled his shoulders nervously.

Thaddeus bit his lip, his mind spinning with ways he

might be able to pull the whole thing off. He had to try something. He couldn't simply let Imogen be dragged into a marriage against her will. And though it might have been boorish of him, he had no intention of letting any other man discover the secrets of her sensuality. The memory of her sweet mouth closed around his cock, drawing the most exquisite pleasure he'd ever felt out of him, threatened to distract him from his vital mission.

He cleared his throat and focused on Oliver. "Can you find her in the ballroom and give her a message that —" His mind raced for an excuse to get her away from her father and Lord Cunningham. With a flash, he stood straighter, his plan forming. "—that you've found a maid willing to repair her gown and she must come with you belowstairs."

Oliver looked doubtful. "Will she come? Moreover, will her father let her come?"

Thaddeus chewed his lip again before inspiration struck a second time. "Tell her that the maid is a highly-accomplished seamstress, that she attended a finishing school for young women wishing to better themselves."

Oliver continued to frown. "Schools like that don't exist for our sort, my lord."

"It doesn't matter." Thaddeus shook his head. "It's a message. She'll know you're speaking for me if you say that."

"Very well, my lord." Oliver sighed, squaring his shoulders. "I'll do it."

"Thank you, friend," Thaddeus told him as he

walked back to the kitchen door. "I swear to you, if I can ever do you a kindness in return, I will."

Oliver nodded before disappearing into the kitchen. That left Thaddeus alone in the mews with his thoughts and anxieties. The plan had to work. There weren't many more opportunities for him and Imogen. Time was running out. He could feel their chances of slipping away to make a life together shrinking with each hour that ticked by.

There was little for him to do but pace the cobblestones of the mews, studying the path he and Imogen would need to run to get away.

"Something wrong, guv'nor?" one of the drivers near the mews's entrance asked.

Thaddeus didn't realize he had an audience in the crowd of carriage drivers waiting for the ball to end, or that they could see through his footman disguise. Then again, servants always seemed to know who everyone of importance was, no matter how they were dressed. "I am attempting to rescue the woman I love from a fate worse than death," he told them.

A chorus of sympathetic hums from the shadows of the carriages and the mews answered him.

"True love," one of the drivers said. "Ain't nothin' better, m'lord."

"Certainly not," Thaddeus agreed. "But my love's blackguard of a father has promised her to an ogre of a man who will use her terribly if the wedding takes place."

Murmurs of horror and indignation rang from every corner of the mews.

"That is why I am attempting to whisk my love away tonight to save her from—"

"Thaddeus." Imogen's desperate whisper stopped his story short.

Thaddeus turned to the kitchen door to find Imogen rushing through, Oliver a few steps behind her. "Imogen." He rushed to her, pulling her into his arms and clasping her tight. He couldn't resist kissing her with his whole heart as the chorus of carriage drivers made sounds of approval and even applauded.

Their celebration was premature, though.

"Ha! I knew some sort of mischief was taking place." Lord Marlowe darted out of the kitchen, Lord Cunningham right behind him.

"I told you, you shouldn't have let the chit go," Lord Cunningham growled.

"I wanted proof of her wickedness," Lord Marlowe said. "This way, we can take care of this pup without witnesses."

Thaddeus thought fast, letting go of Imogen long enough to step in front of her, blocking her from her father and Lord Cunningham. "I won't let you have her," he said, ready to fight.

Lord Marlowe laughed. "You can't do anything about it, boy. She's my daughter."

"I love her," Thaddeus said. "Soon she will be my wife."

Lord Cunningham snorted. "You're wrong there. She will be my wife by Friday."

"Over my dead body," Thaddeus growled in reply.

"That can be arranged," Lord Marlowe said in a sinister voice.

"I don't care how you threaten me—" Thaddeus began.

His words were cut short as Lord Cunningham produced a flintlock pistol from his jacket. How he'd managed to conceal it there was a baffling mystery, but there was no arguing with the weapon.

"Would you rather I kill you or your whore?" Lord Cunningham asked, aiming the gun just over Thaddeus's shoulder.

Imogen yelped and ducked behind Thaddeus even more than she was already concealed. Thaddeus spread his arms to shield her as best he could. "I won't let you hurt her."

"You can't stop me," Lord Cunningham said. "I've got a pistol. Either you'll be dead or she will if you don't bugger off immediately."

"You don't frighten me, Lord—"

With an ear-splitting crack, Lord Cunningham fired. Searing pain shot through Thaddeus's left shoulder. Behind him, Imogen shrieked.

"He's reloading, Herrington," Lord Marlowe said with casual indifference. "You'd better run while you can."

"And why should I?" Thaddeus demanded, clutching his shoulder. "You'll only hurt Imogen if I do."

Lord Marlowe snorted. "Do you think I'd kill the goose that lays the golden egg before that egg has been laid? Or rather, before the goose has been laid." He laughed at his own joke.

"He's right," Imogen sobbed. "You have to run, Thaddeus."

"No, I won't," he said, twisting to face her, though it meant putting his back to Lord Cunningham and giving him a huge target. Thank God pistols took so long to load. "I refuse to leave you."

"You must," Imogen said, weeping. "They won't kill me, but you'll be dead in less than a minute if you stay."

"But—"

"Go! Now!" she ordered, grabbing his shoulders and shoving him toward the shadows of the carriages. "We'll find another way," she added in a harsh whisper.

He didn't want to leave her. Everything within him raged that he was a coward if he abandoned her to her father and Lord Cunningham. If not for her promise— that they would find another way—he would have stayed and faced death. But she was right. They still had time, even if it was barely seconds. He would find another way to rescue her.

"I love you," he said, stealing a kiss as Lord Cunningham growled in victory, his pistol nearly reloaded. "And I will come for you, have faith."

"I do, I do," Imogen wept, then pushed him on.

Cursing in frustration and wishing he had a sword to run Lord Cunningham and Lord Marlowe through with, Thaddeus dashed down the length of the mews.

"Let me help you, guv'nor," the carriage driver near the back of the pack said, hopping down to open the door of his carriage. "Somethin' tells me you need to get away from here faster than you can on your feet, and I'm always one to help true love."

"Thank you, sir."

Thaddeus leapt into the offered carriage, but he hated himself for leaving Imogen to her fate. As soon as he could, he would formulate another plan and rescue her.

Lord Cunningham fired a second time, and Imogen screamed. Several of the horses, still fastened to their carriages, whinnied and reared as much as they could as well. The carriage drivers rushed to calm them and to prevent a stampede, which was exactly the sort of distraction Thaddeus needed to get away. And he did get away. Imogen could have wept with relief for that alone.

There was no time for weeping, though.

"I told you she was a faithless tart," Lord Cunningham growled, lowering his pistol. He stepped closer to her and smacked her hard with the burning barrel of the fired pistol.

Imogen yelped in pain, spilling to the cobblestones. Her heart shattered into a thousand pieces as she let her tears flow freely. How could she possibly allow herself to be married to a brute who would abuse her in that way? And yet, how could she stop it? Everything depended on Thaddeus.

"You were right not to trust her," her father said above her. He didn't even try to help her up, but instead shouted, "Get up, you slut. You're going home and you're staying there until the wedding."

Slowly, her body and face aching, she dragged herself to her feet. One of the maids from the kitchen tried to run out and help her, but Lord Cunningham smacked her as well. That raised a furor with the Mapplethorpe servants.

"We need to get out of here," her father grumbled. "You haven't made any friends in that house."

Lord Cunningham grunted in agreement, but said nothing. As soon as Imogen was on her feet, he grabbed her by the elbow and marched her down the mews, searching for his carriage.

The ride back to her house was painful and brimming with despair. The best Imogen could say about it was that neither her father not Lord Cunningham interfered with her as she huddled in a corner of the carriage, nursing her bruised and stinging head. Lord Cunningham's blow had hit just above her ear, and a small trickle of blood seeped across her hairline and onto her forehead. She reminded herself over and over as her father and Lord Cunningham plotted ways to murder Thaddeus that it could have been worse. It could have been much worse.

As soon as they entered her father's home, she knew it would be much worse. Immediately.

"There's no point in delaying any of this," Lord Cunningham said as he and Imogen's father marched her up the stairs to her bedroom, one on either side, like yeomen at The Tower leading her to the scaffold. "I should just fuck the chit to show her who her master truly is."

A sob escaped from Imogen before she could stop it and she began to shake.

As they passed Alice's room on the way to Imogen's room, Alice poked her head out. "Are you home already?" Her question ended with a gasp when she saw Lord Cunningham.

"Get back in your room and stay there," her father ordered.

Imogen caught Alice's pale expression for a brief moment before their father lunged forward to slam Alice's door on her face. He then continued marching Imogen to her room.

Once they were inside with the door slammed shut behind them, Lord Cunningham began to unfasten his breeches.

"Bend her forward over the bed and spread her legs," he said, his voice gruff. "This won't take but a minute."

"No, no," Imogen wailed, dashing to the other side of the room. But there was no place to hide.

Blessedly, her father looked uncertain. "How do I

know you'll go through with the marriage and the deal we made if I let you have her now?"

Lord Cunningham blew out an irritated breath and let his arms drop to the side, his breeches halfway unfastened. "I would never renege on our deal, Marlowe. You know that."

"Do I?" her father grumbled. "You've reneged on more than a few of the men who tried to marry your daughter."

"That's all water under the bridge, now that Malvis is married off to that buffoon, Ainsley."

"That doesn't change the situation for me," her father said. He paused, rubbing the lower half of his face, and finally went on with, "No. I won't let you sample the sweets before the vows have been made. I must protect my interests. You understand."

Lord Cunningham's face was red with anger, but he grudgingly refastened his breeches. "All right. But I want guarantees that she won't slip out and run off with that whelp."

"Oh, she won't leave this room, I can assure you," her father said.

"How?" Lord Cunningham demanded. "How can you assure me? If you're determined to prevent me from having her in order to protect your own interests, then I want the same."

Her father thought for a moment, studying Imogen as she cowered in the corner, shaking like a leaf. He glanced around the room, then his face lit with wicked inspiration.

"We'll tie her to the bed," he said, marching toward one of the windows and freeing the cord used to hold the curtains open. "You can inspect the knots yourself. I'll give orders that she isn't to be freed until the day of the wedding. Not for any reason."

"Agreed," Lord Cunningham said. "But won't the gown I purchased become badly soiled if it isn't removed?"

Imogen moaned in fear. She could see from the lust in Lord Cunningham's eyes what he had in mind.

"Take it off her, then," her father shrugged as he collected more curtain cords. "But don't try anything as you do."

Imogen tried to run. She tried to fight. But she was helpless against the strength of two grown men, no matter how old they were. Lord Cunningham snatched her from the corner and tore at her gown, laughing as he forcibly removed it. Her father may have warned him against molesting her, but that didn't stop the beast from pawing at her, squeezing her breasts and backside, and doing everything short of invading her as he wrestled her out of her gown and onto the bed on her back.

She gave up fighting and could do nothing but lie there weeping as her father tied her wrists to the bedposts over her head. Whatever hope she had that he would spare her utter humiliation was dashed when Lord Cunningham jerked her ankles apart, tying each to the

posts at the foot of the bed in a way that left her horrifi-
cally exposed. Her father carefully avoided looking at her
like that, but Lord Cunningham drank in the sight.

"I think I'll run off to Mrs. Pettiford's house now," he
growled, rubbing the tented front of his breeches. "Since
you won't let me have that."

"Do whatever you need to do," her father said,
heading for the door. "She'll be yours as of Friday, as soon
as I receive my payment."

They left, but Imogen hardly felt a shred of relief.
She knew her father was cut from the same horrible cloth
as Lord Cunningham, but it hurt far more than she could
bear to have him treat her so shamefully. She wanted to
believe that Thaddeus would swoop in and rescue her,
but hope was hard to cling to.

"Imogen, are you—dear God!" Alice gasped as she
poked her head into the room. She flew to the bed as soon
as she was in the room, grabbing a quilt from the chest at
the foot of the bed and throwing it over Imogen. "Let me
untie you," she said, starting on one of the cords that held
her ankle.

"No." Imogen tugged her ankle away from her sister's
hands as best she could. "Father would only give me
worse if he discovered I'd done something to counter his
wishes. And he'd probably do the same to you."

"But I can't let you just lie here, tied to the bed like
this," Alice insisted.

"Just cover me with the blanket. I'm cold." It wasn't a
lie, but Imogen couldn't bring herself to say, even to her

sister, that she felt so humiliated and defeated. "Thaddeus has promised to rescue me," she said, though her tone conveyed very little hope.

"And I'm sure he will rescue you," Alice said, spreading the quilt over Imogen and tucking it in. The warmth and modesty that the quilt brought made Imogen feel a tiny bit better, but not much. "I'll stay with you as well, as long as Father lets me. I'll stay with you until... until the end."

"Thank you," Imogen sniffed, blinking away her tears. It meant the world to her. She just dreaded what the end might be.

CHAPTER 4

*R*escuing the woman he loved, a woman desperate to be rescued, from a house where the servants were more than willing to help him in every way proved far more difficult than Thaddeus would have imagined. He was able to learn of Imogen's fate from Lord Marlowe's kitchen maid, whom he intercepted on an errand to the market. He was further able to discover when Lord Marlowe would be out of the house from one of the footmen, who found the bastard's treatment of his daughter as infuriating as Thaddeus did. And he was given a full description of the house's layout and the location of Imogen's bedroom by the butler, Mr. Monk.

"I cannot allow you to come through the house to rescue Lady Imogen, my lord," Mr. Monk told Thaddeus as they stood near each other in the park across the street from Marlowe House, pretending to be deeply occupied in their own pursuits. "I must protect the staff from Lord

Marlowe's wrath when he discovers his daughter has flown the coop."

"He will be vicious," Thaddeus admitted with a sigh, studying the imposing, Georgian home. "I have no wish to bring any sort of harm to you or any of the men and women who have risked so much to help with this endeavor."

"We will continue to assist you in any way we can, my lord," Mr. Monk continued. "But for the younger staff especially, to be let go without a reference would be—"

"Devastating," Thaddeus finished.

He was desperate to free Imogen at all cost, but if that cost destroyed the lives of others, it would weigh on his conscience for the rest of his life.

It was that worry that led him to the brainstorm that struck him, giving him the idea for the perfect way to whisk Imogen off right under her father's nose. The plan was so ingenious that he laughed to himself all through Thursday, as he set the wheels in motion, enlisting the help of every other participant he would need to pull off the coup. Everyone he approached with his idea knew the sad fate Lady Imogen had been consigned to, and every one of them was eager to come to Thaddeus's aid.

The last person he needed to inform of the plan was Imogen herself, which was how he found himself climbing a rope ladder of the sort that was found on a ship that had been hung from Imogen's bedroom window by one of Marlowe's footmen. Night had fallen just under an hour ago, and according to Mr. Monk, Lord

Marlowe had gone out with Lord Cunningham to visit various pubs and brothels in celebration of the horrific event that would take place on the morrow. Marlowe wasn't expected back until dawn, which gave Thaddeus all the time he needed.

Imogen's window was cracked slightly, and between the sturdiness of the rope ladder and the help Mr. Monk had provided by oiling the window casing, Thaddeus was able to climb up and open the window almost silently. He could make out Imogen's prone form under a quilt on the bed, but just barely. She didn't stir as he hopped to the floor and closed the window behind him.

It was when he started across the room toward her and the floorboards creaked under his feet that she twisted her head toward him and gasped, "Who's there? Are you a thief? What do you want?"

A relieved smile spread across Thaddeus's face in spite of her fear. "It is a fearsome highwayman, come to kidnap you and steal you away in the dead of night."

Imogen made a sound of shock and relief that dissolved into a tearful, "Thaddeus! You've come for me at last."

"I have, my love," he said, rushing to the bed.

He sought for her head in the dark, and when he found it, he kissed her with all the triumph that had been growing within him since he began setting his plan in motion. She kissed him back, but didn't embrace him. In fact, she barely moved at all. He leaned back, feeling for her shoulders and arms in the nearly black room. With a twist of horror, he discovered that her arms were outstretched, her legs as well.

"Father tied me to the bed," Imogen explained, shame in her voice. "He wanted to be certain I wouldn't escape."

"And you've been here like this since the ball?" Thaddeus growled, furious, as he stood and searched for a lamp to light.

"Alice has snuck in to untie me so that I could use the chamber pot and eat," she explained as he found a match and lit it.

"Why did you not remain untied?" he asked, lighting the lamp.

"Father has suspected Alice is interfering with his disciplinary measures, as he calls it, and has been checking on me frequently." Her voice held a sickened note that infuriated Thaddeus and made him wonder how much Marlowe enjoyed the sight of his daughter tied to her bed. "So Alice and I agreed that I should remain tied as much as possible."

With the lamp finally lit, Thaddeus was able to see Imogen fully. She lay on her back with her arms and legs spread, a quilt covering her. Her wrists and ankles, tied with curtain cords, poked out from the corners of the quilt.

"This is unspeakable cruelty," Thaddeus hissed, returning to the bed, heat burning through him. It wasn't all the heat of anger, however. There was something undeniably arousing about seeing her bound in such a way. In fact, he wanted to peel back the quilt to see what the rest of her body looked like in that position.

"Oh, my," she murmured, squirming slightly under the quilt.

Thaddeus blinked himself out of his lascivious thoughts. "Is something the matter, my heart?"

Now that the room was lit, he could see her cheeks turn a bright shade of pink. "It's just that...." She paused, biting her lip. "It's just that these bonds have seemed like such a miserable humiliation...until now."

"Until now?" His blood began to stir in earnest, jolting straight to his cock. He leaned closer to her, mesmerized by the sudden look of excitement in her eyes. His heart skipped a beat just as it was speeding up, though. He touched a hand to a mean-looking welt just under her hairline. "What happened?"

"Lord Cunningham struck me after you escaped," she admitted, eyes downcast.

"I'll murder him," Thaddeus growled, hatred bursting through him.

"But not now," Imogen said quickly. "He's not here and...and I don't want to think about him. I only want to think about you."

Thaddeus wouldn't have let the matter drop under normal circumstances, but there was something he couldn't resist about having Imogen bound and breathless under him. His mind might have raged for justice, but his body pulsed and ached with need. He couldn't help but study the rest of her form, barely concealed under the thin quilt.

Imogen's breath became shallower, which he could see by the rise and fall of the quilt. "I feel safe now that you are here," she said in a voice as soft as glowing embers. "I didn't understand what Mr. Monk meant when he came in earlier and said my father would be out all night. I didn't realize what he held in his arms and tossed out the window when he was here either."

"It was a rope ladder," Thaddeus told her, reaching for the corner of the quilt near her right wrist. "The servants all helped me to come to you tonight."

"I knew it," she said, her breath quickening even more. "I knew they were keeping a secret. A good secret."

"And now?" he asked, bending to kiss the inside of her wrist just beneath the curtain cord. Blessedly, the cords weren't tied particularly tightly. Imogen could have slipped her hand through if she'd wanted to be free.

"Now," she said, a shiver in her voice as he brushed his lips down her inner arm. "Being tied like this feels...." She didn't seem to have a word for what it felt like, but her intake of breath as he reached the crook of her elbow spoke volumes.

"I am curious about this arrangement," Thaddeus said, feeling more and more like a devil. He rocked back, taking hold of the bottom of the quilt and tugging it slowly. "What must it be like to be tied to a bed, utterly helpless, and at the mercy of whatever wicked-intentioned rogue that might choose to climb through your window."

"Oh," she breathed as the quilt receded from her shoulders and chest. Thaddeus slowed as the upper edge of the quilt slipped over her breasts, watching the way her chest heaved as she gulped for breath, twitching and arching slightly as he teasingly exposed her. She made a desperate mewling sound as the edge of the quilt paused just before revealing her nipples, then let out a moan as he tugged it down. Her nipples were already pert with pleasure, and his cock jumped at the sight of her full, round breasts as they were revealed.

He continued to tug at the quilt, revealing her slim, soft belly and waist, but paused once again when he reached the dark curls between her legs. Instead of revealing her sex, as he longed to do, he pushed off the bed and stood.

"Are you going to leave me like this?" she asked in a high, breathy voice.

"Absolutely not," he answered with a growl, working at the buttons of his jacket.

She watched him undress, her eyes dancing with fire in the scant light of the lamp. He shed his layers quickly, carelessly tossing aside his boots. When he was down to just his breeches, he climbed back onto the bed between her widely-spread ankles and took hold of the quilt once more.

"Thaddeus," she sighed, wriggling her hips as though trying to throw the quilt off.

"My, my," he chuckled. "Someone is surprisingly eager for being tied up." His prick was beyond eager as well and strained against his breeches, begging to be freed.

"I'm yours," she said, her breasts rising as she arched slightly. "I want you so desperately."

"Do you?"

He pulled the quilt down faster than he'd intended to, revealing the tantalizing sight of her sex. With her legs forced wide open, she was on full display. As soon as he'd tugged the quilt down to her thighs, he balled it up and tossed it aside entirely. She moaned and writhed against her bonds, which only highlighted the gaping sweetness of her sex. She was wet and glistening. The pinkness of her folds beckoned to him.

"Such beauty," he growled, reaching for her knees and stroking them with light circles.

She let out an impatient sound, panting as he brushed his fingertips up the inside of her thighs. He took his time, teasing her until she mewled and trembled. All the while, his gaze remained focused on her weeping sex and the carnal need that hardened his cock to the point of madness. She whimpered and writhed with unfulfilled pleasure, letting out sharp, pleading cries as his fingers reached the heart of her sex but only brushed and caressed instead of plunging and satisfying, but the torture he was inflicting on himself was just as acute.

"I want to fuck you so badly," he growled, tracing a finger over the soaking line of her entrance. "I want to thrust my cock hard into this sweet cunny, over and over until you cry out my name as you come."

"Yes," she gasped, arching into his touch.

He kept his touch light, arousing without fulfilling. She twitched against her bonds, seeming even more helpless and at his mercy than she'd been moments before.

He planted his hands on either side of her, leaning over her to bring his mouth to one of her breasts without letting any other part of him touch her. She let out a tight breath as he closed his mouth around her nipple and brushed it with his teeth.

"Oh, God, yes, Thaddeus," she sighed, arching.

He continued to keep his body away from hers, knowing full well how it frustrated her. She sighed and even sobbed as he switched to treat her other nipple to the same teasing as the first, sucking gently and using his teeth and tongue to pleasure that hardened point only.

"Please, Thaddeus," she gasped. "Please."

He leaned back, kneeling between her legs. The sight of her in such a powerful state of arousal, spread, wet, and panting with need, made him feel like a god of pleasure. Something deep and primal within him liked her that way, liked the heady lust of her arousal. It was all for him.

He fumbled with the fastenings of his breeches, pushing them down his thighs and freeing his cock at last. It felt so good to spring upright, hard and alive with pleasure, that he groaned at the sensation. It was even better to see her eyes widen and darken and her mouth fall open, as if she remembered the taste of him deep in her throat. He took himself in hand, stroking carefully from his tip to his balls, caressing his balls as she watched him restlessly.

"I want you," she whimpered, flexing her hips. "Please."

Touching himself brought him dangerously close to climax, especially with the sight of her in such a state. He would remember her this way long into the future. Since her eagerness seemed to increase at the sight of him pleasuring himself, he continued with it, employing every ounce of willpower he had not to come. He could feel the need building at the base of his spine already.

"What would you do if I spent like this?" he asked, his voice rough. "What would you do if I left you aching for release without giving it to you?"

"Then I would ache for you until we were able to be together again," she panted. "I would lie here through the night, on the edge of bursting, unsatisfied."

He could imagine it with perfect clarity, could see her writhing in her bed all night, perhaps trying to bring herself relief but being unable to. She would sigh and squirm with arousal, poised at the brink, nipples hard and sex hot and glistening, waiting for him to make her come. The deeply male part of him wanted that, wanted her to ache for him and to know that he was her master.

An entirely different part of him wanted nothing more than to join with her forever. He wanted to be one with her, to feel her body come apart while lodged deep within her. He wanted to spill his seed in her and stay wrapped in her, two bodies, two hearts, forever one.

That was the part that won out as he surged forward. He couldn't wait another moment. He covered her body with his, guiding himself to the slick opening of her sex and pushing inside of her with last-minute slowness. He wanted her to feel every inch of him stretching and filling her, inch by inch.

She let out a wild cry, even as he met a brief moment of resistance as he breached her maidenhead. For a startling moment, he thought he'd hurt her and paused until she panted, "More, more. Deeper," with such insistence that he couldn't help but obey.

He rocked into her, matching her cries as her body unfurled to accept him. He couldn't help but move, faster and deeper with each thrust, as she squeezed and welcomed him. It was pure bliss to feel her tightness enclose him, to have every nerve in his cock screaming in victory as the friction of their mating urged him on to a release as old as time.

His thrusts grew demanding as the glorious tension in his groin roared to an undeniable climax. Pleasure and light and everything good slammed through him like thunder as he exploded, too overcome with need to pull out and spare her the risk of a child. In fact, knowing that he was spilling inside of her, that his seed might join with her to form new life, made his orgasm so much better than it would have been otherwise. It was only as the initial rush began to subside that he realized her body was throbbing around his in a powerful orgasm of her own.

"Yes," she groaned, radiating heat, her head thrown back in ecstasy. "Thaddeus, yes!"

He continued to move in her until the last of his passion was spent. Then he collapsed atop her, unable to summon the energy even to withdraw from her. His cock felt as though it was exactly where it belonged. His heart was where it belonged as well, with hers, in every way.

It was only when enough sense returned to him that he realized he might be crushing her and he used the last of his strength to pull out and prop himself above her.

"My darling," he panted, bending to kiss her. "My own, dear love." He kissed her again, longer, wondering how long it would be before he was capable of making love to her again. Although, as much as having her tied aroused him, he wanted to have her freely as well. "I love you," he told her, kissing her once more before rocking back.

He pulled up his breeches and refastened them, then climbed off the bed and set about gathering his clothes and dressing.

"I can climb down the ladder," she said, tugging at the cords binding her with a different sort of urgency. "I know I can, if you show me how."

"No," Thaddeus said, returning to the side of the bed. His shirt and waistcoat were on, but his shirt was untucked and his waistcoat unbuttoned. "I didn't come to take you away with me tonight."

"What?" Her eyes were suddenly round with alarm. "Did you come her only to ravish me, then?"

He met her question with a rakish grin. "The ravishing was unintended, but delicious." He leaned in to kiss her startled mouth.

"But I don't understand," she said.

He stepped back, searching for the quilt. He found it on the floor, but before he covered her, he drank in the sight of her body. The bedclothes were rumpled beneath her. In the lamplight, her skin had a flushed glow. Her sex looked as though it had been thoroughly used, which led him to change his mind about simply covering her and leaving.

He searched around for a washstand, found a cloth, wet it, and returned to the bed to clean up the evidence of what they'd done.

"It's too dangerous to carry you away tonight, love," he said as he gently washed her.

She moved as though his ministrations aroused her all over again. "But why?" she asked breathlessly. "Why can I not come away with you right now?"

"I couldn't live with myself if your father fired any of the servants who have risked so much to help me without references," he said.

"So you would leave me to my father's evil plan to spare a handful of servants you don't know?" Panic filled her eyes.

Thaddeus finished his washing, returned the cloth to the washbasin, and returned to cover her. "Do not worry, my darling. I came tonight merely to tell you that I have a fool-proof plan."

"You do?" Hope filled her face once more.

"I do." He bent down to kiss her, tucking her disheveled hair behind her ears. "I will steal you away from the wedding right under your father and Lord Cunningham's noses. They won't know what is happening until it's too late." He kissed her again. "And then we will run away and be safe together forever. Do you believe me?"

She hesitated for only a moment before saying, "I do. I have faith in you. I've always had faith in you."

"Then keep that in the center of your heart," he said, taking one final kiss. A huge part of him hated to leave her. He wanted to stay with her, not just to go another round with her in bed, but to protect her against every manner of evil. Instead, he said, "By this time tomorrow, I swear, we will be free of your father and Lord Cunningham forever. Until then...." He rested a hand on the side of her anxious face, then backed away toward the window. "Know that we will be victorious in the end."

He reached the window, opened it again, and threw his leg over the windowsill, catching his foot in the top rung of the ladder. "I love you, my darling," he said before escaping into the night.

CHAPTER 5

*I*n spite of the fact that her body was thoroughly worn out after her blissful encounter with Thaddeus, Imogen couldn't sleep a wink that night. She alternated between reliving the stunning glory of making love with Thaddeus and the wealth of sinful, delicious feelings that being tied up while he ravished her inspired, and being terrified about what the morning might bring.

She'd only just managed to doze off when her bedroom door cracked open while the night was still deep.

"Who is it?" she whispered, caught between fear of her father or Lord Cunningham and hope that Thaddeus had returned for her after all.

But it was Mr. Monk's voice that whispered, "Go back to sleep, my lady."

He moved to the window, opened it, and proceeded

to drag something back into her room. It must have been the rope ladder Thaddeus has used to reach her room.

"Thank you, Mr. Monk," she said as he stole out of the room with the ladder.

Mr. Monk paused at the door to say, "We are all behind Lord Herrington, my lady, and are offering any help we can."

He slipped out of the room before Imogen could tell him to thank the other servants.

Mr. Monk wasn't her only visitor before the morning light streamed in through the curtains.

"I heard noises coming from your room last night," Alice said as she crept into the room at first light, shutting the door behind her. "Curious noises."

There was no point in hiding anything from her sister. "Oh, Alice, it was wonderful," she sighed, relaxing as Alice undid the cords holding her ankles. "Not even *The Secrets of Love* could have described how wonderful it was."

"It certainly sounded exciting." Alice's eyes lit with mischief and she untied Imogen's other ankle before moving to her wrists. Her grin vanished too quickly. "You should give thanks that Father wasn't home last night. You and Lord Herrington nearly woke the dead with your carrying on."

"I will give thanks that we will never be in this situation again," Imogen said, sitting up and rubbing her wrists once Alice undid the last cord.

Alice sat on the side of the bed with a frown. "Why

did he not simply steal you away when he left? It seems rather rakish to bed you the way he so obviously did and then to fly off into the night."

Imogen climbed off the bed, wincing as she tested her sore muscles and stiff joints. She made her way to the chamber pot behind the screen in the corner of her room, talking as she went. "Thaddeus said that he could not, in good conscience, risk Father dismissing any of the servants because he would most certainly do so without giving them a reference."

"That would ruin them," Alice agreed.

"He says that he has another plan, a better plan." She finished behind the screen, then came out to finish the job at the washbasin that Thaddeus had started the night before. Even cleaning herself reminded her of Thaddeus's touch, arousing her even as she focused on the hope of his words.

"What kind of plan could be better than rescuing you in the dead of night when Father and Lord Cunningham are away and thoroughly distracted?" Alice asked, fetching a robe from the wardrobe and bringing it to Imogen.

"I don't know." Imogen took the robe, wrapping up once she was clean.

Alice arched a doubtful eyebrow. "He refused to whisk you away from the house and he also failed to inform you of his plan?"

Imogen shook her head. "I know you have your doubts, but I trust Thaddeus. I have full faith in him to do whatever is necessary to save me. We will be together forever, I know it. I—"

Her bedroom door swung open before she could go on and her father marched in. He looked first at the bed, and when Imogen wasn't where he assumed she would be, he turned a murderous glare on her and Alice.

"How dare you disobey my orders?" he boomed, crossing the room to them in a few steps. "And you are even worse for turning against me." He grabbed a handful of Alice's loose hair and shook her. "Go back to your room at once, you disobedient slut. Your turn will come soon enough."

"Father, please don't," Imogen pleaded with him.

It was no use. He marched Alice to the door and threw her into the hall. At least one of the maids was there to catch her and comfort her.

When her father was done, he whirled to face Imogen. She expected to be struck again like Lord Cunningham had struck her the other night, but her father's eyes were bloodshot and he was paler than usual, as if he'd enjoyed his evening out with Lord Cunningham a little too much. He didn't have the energy for more than one battle.

"It doesn't matter," he said, as if confirming what Imogen suspected he was thinking. "Put on your wedding gown and come downstairs at once. We leave for the church within the hour."

"So early?" Imogen asked with a gulp. Would Thaddeus have time to execute his plan if they proceeded with things hours before weddings usually took place?

Her father didn't answer. He merely marched out of the room, slamming the door behind him. Imogen glanced from the door to the window, wondering if she had it in her to flee. But Mr. Monk had taken the rope ladder, and she truly did trust Thaddeus, even if everything seemed to be going against them.

She dressed as fast as she could, surprised when one of the maids showed up to help her. It seemed out of character for her father to allow her to have help. He must have been desperate from his night out. That or so confident in his victory that he had become lazy. Either way, Imogen hoped she could use it.

"Where is Alice?" she asked when she met her father in the front hall a short time later.

He already wore his overcoat and hat and seemed even more out of sorts than he had in her room. "She is forbidden to come," he grumbled. "You are forbidden to ever see her again."

Imogen gasped. "But surely...I must return here to gather my things...my book—"

"Once you're in Cunningham's hands, you'll stay there," her father snapped. "He has no need for any of your foolish things."

"But my clothing."

"He'll give you new," her father roared, irritated at being interrupted. "If he wants you clothed at all."

Imogen's mouth dropped open, but she didn't have a

chance to say anything else. Her father grabbed her wrist and jerked her toward the door. Mr. Monk tried to drape her coat over her shoulders, but it fell and her father gave him no time to pick it up. The carriage was waiting, and just as the autumn chill hit Imogen, adding to the shivers that had already overtaken her, he tossed her up into the seat.

They were silent as they rode to the church, just a short distance away. Imogen was too afraid to say a word, and her father pinched his face into a scowl, closing his eyes. Imogen glanced out the window as Mayfair rolled by, searching desperately for any sign of Thaddeus, but there weren't any. The houses were silent, and only servants scuttled about on errands. It was too early for anyone else to be out.

Her dread deepened when they reached the church and Lord Cunningham was waiting for them.

"Not a moment too soon," Lord Cunningham said in a gravelly voice as Imogen's father climbed out of the carriage, practically throwing Imogen to the pavement ahead of him. Lord Cunningham's face was red and his breeches were tented obscenely. "Whatever that whore gave me last night is still working. I need her spread and wet in short order. And I don't care about the wet part."

Imogen shied away from Lord Cunningham with a whimper she couldn't control. She glanced desperately around for Thaddeus, but the street was nearly empty. A young boy raced about on his errands at one end of the row of buildings and a girl with messy hair seemed to be idling her way along on some errand with a basket over her arm. Thaddeus was nowhere to be seen.

Imogen's father grabbed her arm and yanked her forward. "Right. Rev. Josephs said he'd be ready. Let's get the formalities over with. As soon as the ink is dry on the license and our agreement, you can do whatever you want with this one. I'll even hold her down for you if she makes trouble."

Fear welled up within Imogen. She trembled so much as her father dragged her into the church and down the aisle behind Lord Cunningham that she stumbled twice. She searched the rows of pews for Thaddeus, searched the organ loft, the darkened corners, and even the rafters above them. The church was empty, but for the priest waiting at the front and a young man that must have been some sort of curate helping out. For a moment, Imogen wondered if the curate was Thaddeus in disguise, but the man was shorter and stouter than Thaddeus.

"There you go." Her father pushed Imogen toward Lord Cunningham as they came to a stop at the front of the church. He scowled at the priest. "Get on with it."

"Very well," the priest smiled benignly, coughed once, then opened the book of prayer in his hands. Imogen stared hard at him, trying to communicate her desperation, but the man merely coughed again, hummed, and began the service with, "Dearly beloved, we are gathered here today to witness the union of this man and this woman."

Panic tore through Imogen. Where was Thaddeus? It

was impossible to think that her father and Lord Cunningham had outsmarted him. He must have known the wedding would be early. He was intelligent and cunning, and he loved her far too much to let this travesty continue.

"...which is an honorable estate, instituted by God in the time of man's innocency," the priest went on, interrupted only by another cough.

Prickles broke out along Imogen's skin and her breath came in shallow gasps. It was going to happen. The service was going to proceed, and before Thaddeus could swoop in to save her, she would be married to Lord Cunningham. All she could look forward to then was a wretched life as the unwilling recipient of his prick.

The priest coughed yet again before saying, "First, it was ordained for the procreation of children—"

"And the getting of them," Lord Cunningham added in a sly voice.

The priest answered with a cough. At first, Imogen thought he was irritated by the interruption, but instead of going on, he coughed again and pressed a hand to his chest. "—to be brought up in the fear and nurture of the Lord—" he attempted to continue before breaking down once again.

This time, his coughing fit turned into deep, racking gasps. The priest's eyes went wide and he dropped his prayer book. Imogen watched in horror as he began to wheeze and struggle for breath. He clasped both hands to his heart before dropping to the floor.

"Quick," the young curate said, dashing forward. He met Imogen's eyes. "Get him a glass of water." He pointed to the open door to the vestry a few yards away.

Hope as powerful as cannon fire burst through Imogen. This was it. This was Thaddeus's plan. She broke away from Lord Cunningham—who, along with her father, had rushed forward and crouched by the priest to see what was going on—and dashed for the vestry.

Her hopes proved founded as soon as she whisked through the door. Thaddeus was waiting there for her, just out of sight of the chapel.

"Quick." He grabbed her hand and pulled her along to a door at the other side of the room. "We haven't got much time. They'll realize something is wrong when you don't come back."

"Too right we will," her father's angry voice boomed behind them.

Imogen yelped, putting everything she had into dodging through the back corridors of the church along with Thaddeus. It shocked her how quickly her father had figured out Thaddeus's plan. She held onto Thaddeus with a grip like iron as he took her out into the alley behind the church and on.

"Stop, you bastard," her father shouted as he chased them. "You won't get away with this. You have nowhere to go." He was far too close for Imogen's liking. The only thing she and Thaddeus had in their favor was that her father was older and worn out from the night before.

"Follow me," Thaddeus said over his shoulder as they darted down the narrow path between two buildings that appeared to lead back to the main street. "I have a plan and I know where I'm going."

"I trust you," Imogen said, though she was already beginning to wonder if her lungs and her legs would hold up.

They burst out to the street half a block away from the church. Imogen's father still wasn't far behind them. Worse still, Lord Cunningham had made his way out of the church through its front door. He spotted them the moment they charged into the street. Thaddeus tugged Imogen away from the church with purpose in his steps, but Lord Cunningham tore off after them.

"Don't let them get away," her father shouted as Lord Cunningham reached his side.

"I have no intention of letting that whelp make off with my prize," Lord Cunningham said.

Imogen let out a sound of fear, but Thaddeus reassured her with, "It's all right. It's just up ahead. Run with me and be ready for anything."

Imogen would have nodded if she weren't already too terrified to do anything but move. They reached the street just as a carriage charged toward them, but Thaddeus whisked her out of the way of the vehicle before it could do more than whip up a breeze to ruffle Imogen's hair. The carriage slowed her father and Lord Cunningham down a bit. To Imogen's surprise, the girl with the basket who had been loitering by the church rushed forward and began to beat Lord Cunningham with the basket.

The girl was no match for Lord Cunningham, but she and the carriage worked to slow him and Imogen's father down enough that Thaddeus and Imogen were able to put more distance between them. They turned a corner just as the two men started to catch up.

"Keep running and turn left at the end," Thaddeus hissed.

Imogen did as she was told. They turned left down another, narrow alley just as her father and Lord Cunningham reached the first alley. But the tiny space Thaddeus had steered her into turned out to be a dead end.

"No," Imogen gasped, panic rising through her once again at the sight of tight, grey walls every which way she looked.

"Down here," Thaddeus whispered, dashing to what looked like a large crate.

To Imogen's surprise, the crate wasn't a simple box at all. Thaddeus pulled open the top and helped Imogen inside. Instead of a plain, flat bottom, the crate concealed a narrow staircase. There wasn't time for Imogen to be surprised, only for her to charge down the stairs. Thaddeus followed as fast as lightning, closing the crate behind him and flipping some sort of latch.

Once the lid of the crate was closed, it was too dark for Imogen to see where she was. She reached the bottom of the stairs by feel alone, took a few steps back so Thaddeus could descend as well, then pressed her back to what felt like a cold, stone wall.

"Where did they go?" she heard her father say above them. "I could have sworn they came this way."

"There are no windows for them to climb through," Lord Cunningham added. "No doors."

"There must be another alley," her father went on, his voice retreating. "We must have missed it."

Imogen's heart pounded against her ribs as she stood as still as possible, listening with all she had to make certain her father and Lord Cunningham were gone. When absolute silence reigned for a full minute, Thaddeus moved, letting out a breath.

"Come on," he said, reaching for her hand in the thick darkness. She grasped it tight when his found hers. "We have to go on in the dark for a few more yards, but we'll reach a door. Once we pass through that, we can light a lamp to take us the rest of the way along the passage."

"Where does the passage lead?" Imogen asked, staying as close to him as possible as they inched along the pitch-black corridor.

She felt, rather than saw, him grin. "You'll see."

CHAPTER 6

Thaddeus kept a tight hold on Imogen's hand as they wound their way through the initial passage. As soon as they passed through the door, he felt around for the lamp and matches that were always waiting there, and lit the lamp. Imogen drew in a breath at the sight of the plain, tight walls and grabbed his hand again.

"Don't worry," he whispered, replacing the matches and continuing on, holding the lamp aloft. "I know where this passage leads." He paused before glancing sideways at her and saying, "You look stunningly beautiful in that gown."

She let out a sudden, nervous laugh. "I am not certain now is the time for compliments, but thank you." She glanced back the way they'd come.

A smile split Thaddeus's face, born of the confidence he felt, now that they were well on their way to safety.

"Your father and Lord Cunningham are far behind us," he said. "You've no need to worry about them anymore."

"Are you certain?" she asked, swaying closer to him as they turned a corner and continued on. The sound of conversation from a house they passed by must have frightened her, but the passage had no access to that house.

"I thought you trusted me, love," Thaddeus teased her.

She let out a breath, letting her shoulders drop a bit. "I do. I truly do."

They continued on in silence. The passageway was extensive and used for a variety of purposes. It had several side paths and formed a vast network under Mayfair. Thaddeus was convinced it must have originally been built by smugglers or conspirators, considering which houses it connected, but he was grateful they'd built it.

After about ten minutes of walking, they reached a doorway that stood open to a large, clean cellar. Imogen hesitated slightly as Thaddeus led her into the cellar, but the moment she spotted his sister-in-law, Lady Caro, she let out a surprised yelp and rushed to her.

"Have you been helping us this whole time?" Imogen asked, throwing herself into Caro's arms.

"We've all been helping you." Rufus stepped into the cellar from the hall with a smile. "And we'd like to continue to help you, if you'd care to come out of this dank cellar and up to where we have tea prepared."

Thaddeus crossed the cellar to shake his brother's hand. "Thank you for everything," he said, thumping his back.

"You're not completely out of the woods yet," Rufus said as they headed through the downstairs hall and up to the ground floor of Caro's school.

Imogen glanced around with wide eyes, laughing as soon as she realized where they'd ended up. They were both mobbed by a dozen young ladies, the pupils of the school, all of whom seemed to be talking and asking questions at once as they escorted Imogen and Thaddeus into the large hall that served as a dining room and auditorium when needed.

"Enough questions," Caro told the young ladies, gesturing for them to return to their seats at the room's two, long tables, where it appeared breakfast was in the process of being served. "Let Lady Imogen and Lord Thaddeus catch their breaths and decide what to do next."

"It's so romantic," one of the young ladies said.

"It's like some sort of fairy tale," another agreed.

Thaddeus exchanged a wry grin with his brother as they walked toward the head table at the far end of the room. "Too many of those fairy tales ended badly," he said, still a bit on edge.

"Which is why we need to get the two of you on to Gretna Green as quickly as possible," Rufus agreed.

"Yes, Gretna Green," Imogen said, letting go of Caro

and rushing to take Thaddeus's hand. "The sooner we are married, the safer we will be."

"I agree," Thaddeus said, his heart filling with pride at how brave she was.

"It might not be as easy as you think," Caro cautioned them as they reached the head table and sat.

The new system Caro had put in place at her school required the students to take turns serving at table. Thaddeus had a feeling that the young ladies had fought each other for the pleasure that morning. At least half a dozen young women with bright, curious eyes and pink cheeks hovered around the table, pouring tea, serving egg tarts, and generally getting in each other's way more than they helped each other.

"Father and Lord Cunningham won't let me go so easily," Imogen agreed with Caro as she picked up her over-filled cup of tea and one of the three tarts the young ladies had plopped on her plate. "It will be a matter of pride to both of them."

"I won't let them lay a hand on you," Thaddeus said, then bit into a tart.

"We shouldn't delay, even for a moment," Imogen went on. "They're out there searching for us right now. The sooner we hire a carriage and are on our way north, the better."

"You're right about that," Rufus said, "but I have another idea."

"Another idea besides Gretna Green?" Thaddeus asked.

"No, you still need to head north, but—"

"They're here!"

The shout from the hallway echoed through the dining hall, sending everyone into chaos. The young ladies jumped up from their tables as though they were about to be called to war. Thaddeus nearly choked on the sip of tea he'd just taken. He launched to his feet, bringing Imogen with him.

"They can't have traced us here so quickly," he said, stepping away from the bench and glancing around desperately.

"I won't go back with them," Imogen said, both fear and ferocity in her expression. "I won't leave you." She clung to Thaddeus's arm.

"Ladies, please settle," Caro called over the buzzing room. "This ruse depends entirely on your ability to act as though nothing is wrong."

A chorus of agreement and the scrape of benches against the floor as the ladies resumed their seats, their breakfasts, and their conversations followed. Rufus darted toward a sideboard against the back wall.

"Help me move this," he told Thaddeus, who leapt into action.

The sideboard concealed a hidden door in the wall, which opened with a snap once the sideboard had been moved far enough forward. Thaddeus grabbed Imogen's hand and yanked her into the dark passage, his heart pounding in his throat. Rufus shut the door behind him, the scrape of the sideboard being replaced followed, and less than a second later, Lord Marlowe's voice boomed from the far end of the room, "Where are they?"

Imogen let out an anxious squeal and pressed herself against Thaddeus in the dark passage.

"We're safe," he insisted. "Rufus and Caro won't betray us."

"I demand to know where my daughter is this instant," Lord Marlowe continued to bellow.

Two sets of heavy footfalls grew closer as Thaddeus assumed Lord Marlowe and Lord Cunningham marched into the room.

"What the devil is the meaning of this interruption?" Rufus shouted. His voice was far enough away that Thaddeus guessed he—and likely Caro as well—had dashed away from the sideboard as fast as they could to avoid as much suspicion as possible.

"This school is notorious," Lord Cunningham shouted in return. "And the two of you are as bad as bad can be."

"I fail to see what that signifies," Caro said. Her voice was now far enough from Thaddeus and Imogen's hiding place that Thaddeus guessed the confrontation was happening in the middle of the dining hall.

"You're hiding them, aren't you?" Lord Marlowe continued. "I swear by everything I hold dear, I will bring this wicked establishment down around your ears if you do not hand my daughter over this instant."

"She is my bride," Lord Cunningham added. "I will not be jilted at the altar."

"Whether you are or are not," Rufus said, "it is none of our concern. My wife runs this school as a home for young ladies who have been through distressing circumstances and wish to better themselves. Men like you are certainly not allowed here. I demand you leave at once."

"I am not leaving without my bride," Lord Cunningham bellowed.

"Then I shall be forced to remove you," Rufus shouted, just as loud.

"Search the place, if you'd like," Caro said above both men. "You'll see that your daughter is not here."

"Yes, we will search the place," Lord Marlowe said, a note of triumph in his voice. "We'll search it from top to bottom, and when we find my daughter and that bastard who absconded with her, we'll call in the authorities."

"By all means. Call them in now, if you'd like." Rufus's voice retreated as he spoke.

There was a pause, then the sound of benches being scraped back once more and a dozen young women bursting into murmurs and excitement.

"What if they find the secret passages?" Imogen whispered, clinging more tightly to Thaddeus.

"I doubt they will," Thaddeus said. "They are a closely-guarded secret."

All the same, Thaddeus grasped Imogen's hand and felt his way along the passage until they heard Lord Marlowe and Lord Cunningham's voices again.

"This is an outrage," Lord Marlowe was shouting uselessly. "Aiding and abetting fugitives is a crime."

"I'll sue if we find them," Lord Cunningham growled.

Thaddeus listened as furniture was overturned and thrown about. Rufus and Caro protested, but he could tell there was a theatrical note in their complaints. They knew full well that Lord Marlowe and Lord Cunningham would find nothing, no matter how destructive their search.

It was a good half hour before the two horrible men barged their way through every room in the establishment. Thaddeus and Imogen followed their progress through the passageways as far as they could. The more frustrated the two men became, the more confident Thaddeus felt.

"Face it, Marlowe," Lord Cunningham said at last. "They're not here. We've wasted time chasing them. They could be halfway to Gretna Green by now."

So the two pricks knew that he and Imogen would be heading to Gretna Green. Thaddeus frowned at the prospect as they made their way back down to the dining hall through the passageway. The roads would be searched. Every carriage on its way north as well. Perhaps he should have thought through his plan a little harder.

He had made up his mind to impose on Caro's hospitality a little longer and to keep Imogen hidden at the school by the time the sideboard in the dining hall scraped aside and Rufus opened the door to let them out.

"They're gone," Rufus said, gesturing for them to step forward and resume their place at the table.

"Will they come back?" Imogen asked, still frightened.

"I doubt it," Caro said, pouring Imogen a fresh cup of tea. "Before they left, they were listing all the places they believe the two of you would be hiding."

"I predict they will spend the rest of the day looking for you," Rufus added. "But they won't come back here."

"Good," Thaddeus said. "I've been thinking that we should probably stay here for a while instead of heading straight up to Gretna Green."

"That's a preposterous idea," Rufus said, all business. Thaddeus opened his mouth to protest, but Rufus continued with, "But traveling by road is an equally preposterous idea."

"How else does one reach Scotland?" Imogen asked. "I know the roads are bad, but—"

"By sea," Thaddeus said as the truth hit him. He blinked, then turned to his brother. "You plan for us to sail up the coast to Scotland rather than going by land."

"It's the best possible way," Caro said as though she had known of the plan all along and agreed.

"Your father and Lord Cunningham will not give up trying to catch you and bring you back until they have a solid reason to give up," Rufus told Imogen.

"Like proof of our marriage," Thaddeus said.

Imogen bit her lip, looking more distressed than ever. "I fear that even then they won't give up. Not with their pride in ruins."

"It doesn't matter." Thaddeus turned to Imogen,

taking her hands. "We'll escape. We'll board the next ship heading anywhere but here. We can make a new life together, in America, in Australia, in China, for all I care. We'll go as far away as possible so that they never find us."

Imogen smiled at him, her expression equal parts gratitude and fear. "I still believe they will chase us."

"Every man has his limits," Rufus said. "I cannot believe that men like your father and Lord Cunningham will spend the rest of their lives in pursuit of you."

"They'll move on to their next, horrid scheme," Caro agreed.

"But traveling to Scotland by ship will provide you with other advantages," Rufus went on. "The captain I plan to introduce you to will be only too happy to take you wherever you want after your marriage. He's a good man."

"And he's ready to sail with the tide later today," Caro said.

"Today?" A surprising twist of alarm filled Imogen's eyes.

"This is perfect," Thaddeus said, his relief a sharp contrast to her shock. "We can head down to the water-front immediately and board the ship. I doubt your father and Lord Cunningham will think to look for us there."

"But—" Imogen stammered. She shook her head. "No, I cannot leave today, this instant."

"Why not?" Caro asked. "If it is clothing that

concerns you, I'm certain my pupils will give you whatever you need."

Instant agreement from the dozen young ladies was followed by a scramble to leave the dining hall, probably in search of garments to gift to Imogen.

"That isn't it," Imogen said, loud enough to stop a few of the young ladies in their tracks. She turned back to Thaddeus, Caro, and Rufus. "No, I cannot leave London without seeing Alice first. I must tell her what is going on. I have to explain it to her."

"I'm certain she would understand," Rufus said.

"No." Caro rested a hand on his arm. "I'm afraid you do not understand the bonds of sisters, my dear. Especially since poor Lettuce was ripped apart from them so horribly."

"Yes, you're right," Imogen said, blinking away tears. "I must see Alice before I go. And I must retrieve my portion of *The Secrets of Love.*"

"The secrets of what?" Rufus looked confused.

A sly grin tugged at the corners of Caro's mouth. "Never you mind, my darling," she said, patting Rufus's arm. "You must go to Alice."

Thaddeus saw that he wouldn't be able to convince Imogen to follow any other course of action. He didn't really want to convince her. He would do anything for her, even something this dangerous.

"We should go at once," he said with a nod. "While your father and Lord Cunningham are still out searching for you." When Rufus frowned at him, Thaddeus went on with, "We are far more likely to be able to get in and out of Marlowe House without being seen, say goodbye to Alice, and collect whatever Imogen wants to take with her if we go while the search is still underway."

"But the servants," Rufus began.

"The servants have been helping us every step of the way," Thaddeus said. "I believe they will continue to help."

"Then you are right," Caro said. "You must go at once." She stepped away from the table, gesturing for Thaddeus and Imogen to come with them.

"I'll write down the name of the ship you should seek out at St. Katherine's Dock," Rufus said, darting ahead of them. "But whatever you do, don't delay."

Thaddeus didn't need to be told twice. He took Imogen's hand and marched toward the door. The sooner they slipped in and out of Marlowe House then fled to the ship waiting for them at the river, the better.

CHAPTER 7

*I*mogen's confidence was almost restored by the overwhelming support she and Thaddeus found at Caro's school. For the first time, she was beginning to have more than just faith in Thaddeus's ability to whisk her away from her horrific life and give her everything her heart had ever desired, she was beginning to see how it would be possible.

"We need to be careful making our way back to Marlowe House," she whispered as the two of them rode in one of the school's carriages. "We do not know when Father and Lord Cunningham will return to the house."

"We shouldn't even let this carriage be seen," Thaddeus agreed. "The school's crest on the door will give us away as surely as anything else."

"Then what should we do?" Imogen asked.

Thaddeus's brow knit in thought for a moment. He glanced out the window at the passing houses, then knocked on the ceiling. "Stop," he said, leaning his head out the window slightly so the driver would hear him. "Please stop here."

The driver brought the carriage to a stop along the side of the road, leaning over to say, "Is there a problem, my lord?"

Thaddeus was already opening the door and hopping out when he said, "We don't want the school carriage to be seen by anyone in the house. We'll go the rest of the way on foot."

Imogen scrambled out of the carriage when Thaddeus offered her a hand, her heart knocking against her ribs.

"Won't you be even more obvious traveling on foot, my lord?" the driver asked.

"Not if we sneak in the back way," Imogen said, taking Thaddeus's hand. It gave her a thrill to think that she would be the one taking charge for a change. "Thank you for everything," she called over her shoulder to the driver as she and Thaddeus hurried on.

They dashed to the end of the street, then crossed over into the mews that led behind her father's house. It was past midday, and the mews were buzzing with activity. Scullery maids and hall boys from the grand houses on either side of the mews rushed about, emptying slops and dirty wash water. Maids were beating rugs and a few footmen had taken their shoe polishing out to the open air. Every set of eyes widened as Imogen and Thaddeus raced by, but no one tried to stop them.

"There," Imogen said at last, when they'd reached the far end of the row. "That one is ours."

Thaddeus grinned. "I remember. I would recognize that wall I climbed up any day."

Imogen giggled at the memory of Thaddeus's daring stunt, then blushed and heated all over as everything they'd done that evening flooded back to her. She would have given anything to feel the press of his body against hers again, to taste the salt of his skin. He'd done so much to her while she lay helpless and bound beneath him, but she wanted to do so many things to him in return. There were parts of him that she'd glimpsed in the flickering lamplight that she wanted to explore for hours in all the ways *The Secrets of Love* had suggested.

Thoughts of her beloved book and the sisters who had the other pieces stopped her thoughts from spiraling too far out of control. "We have to find a way in that doesn't put the servants in a dangerous position," she said as Thaddeus started forward.

Thaddeus paused and twisted back to face her. "Can't we just walk in and steal up to your room to fetch your things? I believe there isn't a soul in your father's house who wouldn't help us."

Imogen bit her lip. "Father's valet, Mr. Barker, could cause trouble."

"Is he loyal to your father? More than Mr. Monk?"

"I think he's more afraid than loyal," Imogen said, marching forward and past Thaddeus. She had a feeling that her father's servants already knew they were there, even if none of them were pouring out the kitchen door to greet them. "He's the only one in the house who might report back to Father that we were here, but even that is bad enough."

"Then we'll need to be careful," Thaddeus said.

He took the lead once more, pausing outside of Marlowe House's kitchen door to peer inside. Whatever hope Imogen had that they could sneak in and out unnoticed was dashed immediately as Dotty, the kitchen maid, came striding out. Her thoughts must have been miles away, because she nearly ran headlong into Thaddeus. She let out a shriek, but quickly clapped a hand over her mouth.

"It's only us, Dotty," Imogen said, rushing forward.

"Oh, my lady," the wide-eyed maid said, going pale. "The house has been in such a state since you left. We... we heard you'd run off and disappeared."

"Not quite disappeared," Imogen said. "We need to see Alice." With a flash of inspiration, she asked, "Can someone be sent to fetch her? And to tell her to bring a few of my things down?"

Dotty wrung her hands in her apron. "No, my lady. Lord Marlowe locked her in her room and threw away the key. None of the servants are to go above stairs at all, let alone into her room."

"No one is allowed above stairs?" Thaddeus seemed encouraged by the idea.

"That's what Lord Marlowe said," Dotty whispered.

"Is he here?" Imogen asked.

Dotty shook her head. "He came flying in over an hour ago, as angry as I've ever seen a man, my lady. He gave us all a heap of orders, then he and that terrible Lord Cunningham left again."

"But this is perfect," Thaddeus said, his grin widening and calculation lighting his eyes. "If no one is upstairs, we can slip into Alice's and your rooms and get what we need, then be off and on our way to the docks as fast as lightning."

"If we can get past Mr. Barker and the others," Imogen said.

"Mr. Barker is in a right state, my lady," Dotty whispered. "He keeps wailing about duty and being sacked."

"Can you keep him and the rest of the staff distracted in the servants' hall while we slip past?" Imogen asked.

Dotty looked beyond pleased to be asked to do something so important. She nodded quickly, her cheeks pink with pride. "I can, my lady. For you, I can do anything."

Dotty whipped around and disappeared back into the house. Imogen reached for Thaddeus's hand, squeezing it and wondering what Dotty would do and how she would know when the time was right for her and Thaddeus to dash into the house.

Her answer came moments later in the form of an almighty crash. Several people raised a cry immediately after, and Thaddeus started into the house, tugging Imogen with them.

"You useless clod! Look at the mess you've made," the cook, Mrs. Folger, was bellowing in the servants' hall as

Imogen and Thaddeus slipped into the kitchen. "Now we'll all have to clean it up."

Even with the commotion in the servants' hall, it was a surprise that the kitchen was completely empty. Pots boiled away on the stove and the scent of roasting meat wafted from the oven. Someone should have been minding the food, no matter what was going on in the other room. That alone convinced Imogen that, within the space of seconds, Dotty had enlisted Mrs. Folger's help to keep everyone distracted.

Indeed, when she and Thaddeus tiptoed past the doorway to the large room where the servants ate their meals and did their handiwork, the scene they caught a brief glimpse of was nearly comical in its intensity. A massive tureen of stew had crashed to the floor, and every servant in the house seemed to be trying to clean it up at once. In the middle of the group was Mr. Barker, who everyone seemed to be trying to distract. At one point, Mr. Monk straightened and looked right at Imogen. His eyes went wide, and he gestured for her to hurry on her way.

It was hard for Imogen to keep herself from laughing at the madness of it all as she and Thaddeus tore up the stairs and through a doorway into the main part of the house. She didn't dare tell Thaddeus how funny and encouraging the thought of the whole thing was, or even where they were going as she took him down the hall to the grand staircase and up to the first floor, where her and Alice's rooms were.

"I don't think Alice would mind if we gathered my things before going to see her," she finally whispered once they were safe in Imogen's room.

"Tell me what to pack and I'll get a bag ready while you speak with her," Thaddeus said, dashing to the wardrobe.

"I don't care what we bring," she said, racing to the table beside her bed to snatch up her section of *The Secrets of Love*. "The more we carry with us, the harder it will be to make a run for it."

"You're right," Thaddeus said, finding a small sack tucked beneath her gowns in the wardrobe. "But surely a few small items won't slow us down too much."

As he started stuffing the sack with underthings from the wardrobe's drawers, followed by a couple of her gowns, shuffling came from the other side of the wall that connected Imogen's room to Alice's.

"Is that you, Imogen?" Alice's muffled voice came through the wall.

Imogen dashed to the wall and laid her hands on the paper, as if she could reach through to embrace her sister. "It is," she said. "Oh, Alice, I'm so worried about you."

"You are worried about me?" Even through the wall, Imogen could hear the incredulous shock in her sister's voice. "I've been terrified for you since Father came home and said the wedding had been ruined, then locked me in here. What happened?"

"Thaddeus rescued me from the church," Imogen said, sending Thaddeus a broad smile as he came forward to take *The Secrets of Love* from her and slip it into the sack. "I knew he would save me. He is a hero of the finest order."

"I would do anything for you, my love," he said, then stole a kiss that had Imogen's head spinning.

"But why are you here?" Alice asked through the wall, unable to see how distracted Imogen had suddenly become.

Imogen dragged herself away from Thaddeus's lips to say, "I had to say goodbye to you, to let you know what has happened. And to retrieve *The Secrets of Love*."

"You cannot stay here for a moment longer," Alice urged her. "Father may be out looking for you, but he could return at any moment. He said he would—"

"He would not rest until he saw you dead and you married, as you should be."

Imogen gasped and whipped around to find her father standing in the door to her room, glowering and murderous. She let out a strangled cry and grabbed hold of Thaddeus's arm, clinging to him.

"You won't get away with this," her father said, stalking forward, balling his hands into fists. "I refuse to be humiliated in this manner."

"Where is Lord Cunningham?" Thaddeus asked, standing straight and tall. He blocked Imogen from her father and radiated confidence, as though ready to fight for her honor until the end.

"Cunningham is a fool," her father growled. "He did

not believe me when I said you were soft and would return to the house to see your sister."

"No, Father, no!" Alice shouted, banging on the other side of the wall.

"Silence," her father shouted. Imogen broke out in shivers and Alice went silent.

"Lord Cunningham is not here?" Thaddeus went on, as confident as ever.

"No," her father said. "He—"

He stopped, his eyes going wide as he realized the situation he was in. Thaddeus acted fast, letting go of Imogen and shooting toward her father. He barreled into him, throwing him back and pinning him against the wall. With a sickening crunch, Thaddeus threw a punch that landed square across her father's face. Blood poured from his nose onto his fine suit, but Thaddeus didn't stop there.

He wrenched her father away from the wall, throwing him toward the bed. "You are a cruel and wicked man," Thaddeus shouted. "How dare you use your daughters as pawns in your own game?" He threw another punch that sent her father sprawling across the bed. "What sort of a villain treats his own flesh and blood as cattle?"

He lunged for her father, closing his hands around his neck. Her father made a horrible choking sound.

Imogen shrieked in fear, then found the words to say, "No, don't kill him."

Thaddeus pulled back, letting go of her father's neck but keeping him pinned to the bed. "He would kill me."

"But you are a better man than he is," she insisted. "You are not a murderer."

Thaddeus snarled for a moment, as if he wished he were capable of murder, then slammed his knee into her father's groin. Her father bellowed in pain, clutching his privates and rolling to one side.

"The only reason you will live is because your daughter is an angel," Thaddeus growled. "But I will give you a taste of your own medicine before I rescue Imogen from your villainy forever."

"What are you going to do?" Imogen asked, clasping a hand to her chest, amazed by the turn things had taken. She knew full well that her father was an older man and no match for Thaddeus's youth and strength, but he had always held such sway over her and her sisters.

Thaddeus stared at her father's crumpled form for a moment. A sly grin spread across his face. "I'm going to do the same thing to him that he did to you. I'm going to humiliate him."

He lunged for her father once more. Her father flinched, but instead of attacking him, Thaddeus attacked his clothes. He tore away her father's coat and waistcoat, yanked off his boots, and ripped his shirt and breeches from him. It was disturbing for Imogen to see her father undressed, to see how shriveled and pallid his naked body was. She couldn't look at him for more than a moment and turned away.

Only when Thaddeus growled, "There," did she turn to look again.

Her father was tied to the bed in much the same way she had been and just as naked. He shivered and whimpered, but didn't seem to be able to form the words to beg for help. The man that had terrorized her and her sisters so much looked like nothing more than a weak, old man as he lay there, his wrists and ankles tied, weeping.

"We need to go," Thaddeus said grimly, marching to pick up Imogen's sack of belongings and to take her hand. "The tide won't wait for us."

Imogen followed him into the hall and nearly all the way to the stairs before remembering her sister. "Alice," she said, letting go of Thaddeus's hand and dashing back to her sister's door. She tried the handle, but the door was locked.

"Go," Alice said from the other side. "Get out of here as fast as you can."

"But I don't want to leave you," Imogen said, laying a hand flat on the door.

"You have to go," Alice said. "Whatever you did to Father in there, he will get free in short order. He won't admit defeat yet."

"She's right," Thaddeus sighed, rubbing a hand over his face.

"You have to get away from here as fast as possible," Alice went on. "Run fast and run far."

"I will come back for you if I can," Imogen promised. "We three will be together again someday."

"We will," Alice agreed. "But for now, you have to save yourself."

It was the hardest thing Imogen had ever done to drag herself away from Alice's door and to follow Thaddeus back down through the house. They didn't return downstairs to leave through the kitchen, but rather dashed out through the front door.

The school's carriage was still waiting for them where they'd left it. The driver seemed relieved to have them back again.

"Did you get what you needed?" he asked.

"We did," Thaddeus said as he helped Imogen into the carriage. "Now help us get down to the docks as fast as possible."

"Yes, my lord," the driver said with an energetic grin.

Imogen's heart felt both heavy and ready to take wing at the same time as she climbed into the carriage. The future lay ahead of them, but it was painful to think of Alice and all she was leaving behind.

CHAPTER 8

*I*t came as a shock to Imogen to realize there were vast parts of London that she knew nothing about, in spite of having spent a great deal of her life in the city. The world of the riverfront around St. Katherine's Dock was like an entirely different country. Even late in the afternoon, it was a riot of activity. Tall ships were lined up in marinas and along the water's edge like soldiers waiting for battle. Hundreds of rough, muscled men worked to load and unload cargo. Supporting—and sometimes hindering—them were a second army of warehouse workers, women buying and selling wares—even themselves—children who were either playing, working, or thieving, and animals of every description.

"Surely my father and Lord Cunningham will never find us in this sea of humanity," she said as the carriage stopped in front of an inn that barely looked respectable.

"That is why we have come straight here instead of staying at an inn in Mayfair or some other, less colorful section of town," Thaddeus answered with a wink.

It was a joy to see his spirits so improved. He hopped down from the carriage as soon as it stopped and turned to give Imogen a hand down. Imogen was still dressed in her wedding gown, and more than a few of the passersby stopped to gape at her. They probably wondered what a lady as refined as she was could be doing in the rough and tumble docklands, even though Imogen didn't feel particularly fine at the moment. She was exhausted and not as fresh as she had been when the day began, what felt like a lifetime ago.

"If we're lucky," Thaddeus said as he hefted her bag over his shoulder and offered his arm to escort her into the inn, "the innkeeper will see fit to have a bath brought up to our room."

"Our room?" Imogen's eyes went wide.

He sent her a teasing grin as they ducked under the low doorway and into the noisy common room of the inn. It was already bustling with dockworkers who had come in for a meal and travelers waiting for their ships to depart.

"Can I help you, sir?" A middle-aged man with a jovial look about him stepped forward from the bustle.

"Yes. A room for me and my wife, if you please," Thaddeus said. He didn't so much as flush at the lie of her being his wife. Then again, if all went as they planned, she would be his wife within a week. "And a bath, if possible," he added as the innkeeper gestured for them to follow him.

As it turned out, in spite of the rough-and-tumble look of the docks in general, the inn Thaddeus had chosen for them to rest in while waiting for news of the ship that would take them to Scotland was clean and efficiently run. Imogen began to feel as though they might finally make their escape as she settled into a chair at the tiny table the room they were given held. A cheery maid brought them hearty stew and good bread for supper while another maid worked to prepare a bath in a large, brass tub.

"I might be able to get used to this sort of life," Imogen said with a smile, helping herself to a sip of Thaddeus's beer.

"A life on the run with your life in peril at every turn?" Thaddeus laughed.

"No, a life with hot meals served with a smile and warm baths brought up to my room," she laughed in return.

Thaddeus blinked at her, his mirth fading. "Don't you have those things at home?"

Imogen shook her head as she took a bite of bread. "Father never lets us bathe in our own rooms and he says there's no point in heating the water for women. And our servants rarely smile."

Thaddeus blew out a breath and rubbed a hand over his face. "Perhaps we weren't doing any of your servants a favor by protecting them from being sacked."

Imogen sighed and mulled over the problem while finishing her bread. "Either way, it is all in the past now."

"As soon as the boy I sent out discovers where our ship is and when it sails, we'll finally be safe," he added.

"How long will it take him to find out?"

Thaddeus shrugged. "There's no telling. Not long."

"What should we do until then?" Her heart sped up as she glanced past Thaddeus to the cozy bed tucked in a corner of the room. It was madness for her to even think of such things when they were in the middle of their escape, but once the idea took hold, it refused to go away.

Thaddeus seemed to know what she was thinking without having to turn to see what she was staring at. His eyes sparkled and his mouth curved up in a sensual smile. "We'll take a bath, of course."

"Oh." Imogen's shoulders drooped. She had forgotten about the bath, even though it steamed at the other side of the room, near the fireplace. Baths were always cold, hurried affairs. It seemed like such a burden when there were far more interesting things they could be doing.

But when Thaddeus finished his meal, stood, and extended a hand to her to help her up, the delicious, pulsing feeling in her belly returned instead of going away.

"Let me help you off with your gown," he said, mischief radiating from him.

"If you think it would be more efficient," she said, a catch in her voice.

"Much more efficient." His voice had taken on a deep, purring tone.

He gestured for her to turn around, then tugged at the ties holding her gown closed right away. Imogen sucked in a breath at the brush of his hands. She gasped outright as he leaned in to kiss the crook of her neck lightly.

"Oh, my," she sighed, tingling all over with need.

Thaddeus merely laughed deep in his throat, a sound that was almost sinister, and pushed her bodice off of her shoulders to reveal more skin. His lips followed where her gown fell away, brushing and nipping and teasing her until a fire lit in her core that spread through her. He tugged at her gown the way he had tugged at the quilt that covered her just the night before, inching it slowly down her arms and chest.

"Yes," she sighed, eager to give him everything and more. "Yes, my love."

He inched away, chuckling. "I didn't ask a question."

She twisted in his loose embrace, wriggling out of her gown and letting it drop to her feet as she did. "You didn't need to," she told him, then slid her arms over his shoulders.

It was her turn to be bold. She swayed into him, bringing her mouth to his and kissing him with all the passion that had been locked within her for so long. He accepted her eagerly, closing his arms around her waist and pressing her flush against him. With only her chemise, stays, and stockings on, she was able to lift her leg against his, arching her hips into him and hinting at all the things she wanted him to do to her.

Their kiss was so ardent and so distracting that Imogen forgot everything else, until Thaddeus said, "Our bath awaits."

It took a moment for the haze of her lust to clear enough for her to blink and ask, "Our bath?"

Thaddeus grinned, stepping back enough to begin unbuttoning his jacket. "You didn't think I was going to let you enjoy that scrumptious bath all by yourself, did you?"

The thrill of all that his question implied swirled through her. As he shrugged out of his jacket and started on the buttons of his waistcoat, she pulled at the ties of her stays. "The tub is so small," she said, glancing past him to where the water was only barely steaming.

"We'll make do," he said, flickering one eyebrow up.

It took far less time for both of them to undress than Imogen would have imagined. All she could think about was how they might take advantage of their bath. She finished with her clothes first and skipped over to the tub, stepping into the water. It lapped against her calves, but as nice as it was, it was nothing to the sight of Thaddeus shucking his breeches. His male part was already excited and stood out prominently. Imogen bit her lip, remembering the salty, musky taste of him as she'd swallowed him at the Mapplethorpe ball. That seemed like a lifetime ago, and she was eager to repeat the whole experience.

"You're beautiful," she said, only barely able to find her voice as he strode closer to her. "I want to touch you in so many ways."

"And I want to ravish you until you're weak and panting my name," he said as he stepped into the tub with her.

It really was too small for both of them, but he sat first, then drew her down to straddle him in the cramped space. Water splashed freely over the sides, especially when he drew her ankles up and placed them over the lip of the tub. The result was that, once again, she was in an awkward, exposed position and completely at his mercy.

"I'm not certain this is the most efficient way to get clean," she panted, barely able to think, let alone speak.

"Bathing is not my first priority," he said, lifting handfuls of water and pouring them over her shoulders.

She gasped as he repeated the gesture. He seemed mesmerized by the way the water trickled over her breasts, her nipples going hard at the contrast of warm water and cool air. It was even better when he shifted from merely pouring water over her to caressing her breasts and dragging his thumbs over her nipples, as though he were a sculptor, forming her out of wet clay. He managed to clean away the dirt of the day while making her feel anything but clean on the inside.

"Yes," she sighed again, relaxing against the back of the tub and giving in to the sensations he was arousing in her.

"I didn't ask a question this time either," he said with a growl in his voice.

"You don't need to. The answer will always be yes."

"Even if I do this?"

He pinched both of her nipples, harder than she would have expected. She squealed, but equally unexpected was the deep pleasure she felt at the brief moment of light pain. It was as though bolts of magic shot straight to her sex from the point of his teasing, making her restless and eager for more.

He gave her more by trailing his hands across her belly under the level of the water and along her inner thighs. She let out a sound of desire before she could stop herself. His answering hum of approval only aroused her more. He stroked her inner thighs, parting her hips farther as his fingers teased closer and closer to her sex.

The anticipation was sweet torture. She gripped the edge of the tub, arching her hips toward him and encouraging him to take whatever he wanted from her. His thick staff pressed against her backside in a surprisingly tantalizing way. She caught herself wondering what it would feel like if he took her in the most scandalous way possible. It was almost unimaginable, but if that part of him felt as good inside of her that way as it did in the usual way, she would submit to whatever liberties he wanted to take with her. She would let him have her in any way he could dream up.

Her heated fantasies were brought back down to earth as he brushed his fingers over the opening of her sex. She hadn't realized that she'd closed her eyes, but they popped open as she sucked in a breath, her body tensing in anticipation of so much more.

"You like that," he said in a passion-rough voice.

"I like everything you do to me," she sighed, moving her hips to pleasure herself against his hand.

"Even this?" he asked, sliding a finger deep inside of her.

She moaned at the pleasure his invasion gave her as she squeezed his finger. "Yes."

"And this?" he added a second finger, moving in and out of her.

She wriggled and bore down on his fingers. "Oh, yes."

"This?" His voice grew heavier as he added a third finger.

Something shifted within her. The simple, teasing passion they'd been sharing took on a hotter, more sensual, and far more dangerous hue. His fingers stretched her, and she found she wanted more. She wanted things that felt shocking and scandalous, and she wanted them desperately.

"Yes," she panted. Her breasts bobbed at the surface of the water as she jerked into his movements.

A lusty fire filled his eyes as he fit his fourth finger inside of her. Part of her didn't think she could bear the fullness of almost his entire hand within her, but another part found it unspeakably delicious. She cooed and whimpered as he thrust in and out of her, stretching her to the edge of her tolerance as a powerful orgasm crashed in on her. The sensation was strange and beautiful and slightly frightening, but she gave into it, tossing her head back, arching her breasts up, and throbbing around his hand as he pleasured her.

"Christ, Imogen," he growled. When she opened her eyes, he was watching her body as she came. His face was flushed and he looked as though he were seeing a wonder of the world. He moved both hands up to cradle her wet breasts, her chest heaving in an attempt to catch her breath.

Her passion might have been ebbing, but his was raging as hot as ever. In one, swift movement, he stood, carrying her out of the tub with him as though she weighed nothing. She was instantly alive again as he stepped toward the bed, but he stopped halfway there.

"I can't wait," he said, letting her down to her feet.

She wasn't certain she had the strength in her legs to stand after the shattering orgasm he'd given her, but as it turned out, she didn't have to. He twisted her in his arms to face away from him, stepped over to the table where the remnants of their supper still sat, and bent her forward. She managed to grip the edge of the table for balance just in time as he lifted her hips and slammed into her.

It was fierce and hot. His thick cock pounded deep within her in a different way than he had before. He took her in what would have been a savage way, except that she adored every moment of it. Her breasts rubbed hard against the tabletop as he jerked into her, faster and harder, his breath coming in loud, desperate cries. The ache in her core flared and pleasure spilled through her all over again as he thrust. She was so open to him, so much at his mercy, and it felt divine.

In no time, she was sighing and crying along with him as he drove home. His fingertips pressed hard into her hips, and she could feel the tension building within him, even as it reached towering heights in her. She was so primed and ready that as he cried out and thrust deep within her, spilling his seed against her womb, she came so powerfully it felt as though she would be consumed by pleasure. She didn't know where she ended and he began as her body squeezed him, drawing every last drop of him into her.

At last, he groaned with satisfaction and sagged against her, his body curled over hers. They struggled to catch their breaths and to return to the world around them. He reached to cradle her breasts as they simply stood there, braced against the table, his softening staff still inside of her.

"Yes," she managed to say at last, arching her hips toward him. "Even that, yes."

He started to laugh, his arms tightening around her in an embrace, but a knock at the door silenced them both.

"My lord," a young voice said from the other side of the door.

Imogen tensed, both horrified and aroused by the idea of whoever it was opening the door and finding them in their current position.

The door didn't open, but the voice continued. "My lord, I found the *Lucky Devil*, as you asked. Captain Devereux plans to sail in less than two hours. He urges you to board the ship as soon as possible."

"Thank you," Thaddeus called over his shoulder. "We will be down shortly."

Footsteps moved away from the door. Imogen relaxed slightly, wondering how long the young man had been outside their door and what he had heard.

Thaddeus must have been thinking the same. He chuckled and rested his head on Imogen's shoulders for a moment. His hips flexed into hers, and for half a second, she wondered if he was coming alive for a second go already. But, at last, he withdrew from her and righted himself. She struggled to stand straight and gather her wits about her as well.

"We need to hurry to make it to the ship on time," he said, still somewhat breathless. His expression filled with renewed desire as he drank in the sight of her pink and sated body when she turned around, leaning against the table for balance. "And once we're safe and sound aboard that ship, we'll go at it again. And again and again," he added as he crossed to the pile of his clothes on the floor. "And again." He laughed.

"Yes," Imogen sighed. Not even *The Secrets of Love* could have prepared her for the delight she knew she would forever find in Thaddeus's arms.

haddeus's spirits were running high as he led Imogen back down through the inn, her sack of belongings slung over one shoulder. He stopped only briefly to pay the innkeeper a bit extra for everything he would have to clean up in the room they'd used. He felt as though he had quicksilver in his veins as he dashed out to the street with Imogen, following the lad who had informed them of the *Lucky Devil's* plans through the inn room's door. Perhaps every grand adventure was better when it began with a thorough round of tupping.

"Which way to the Lucky Devil?" he asked the young man who had knocked on their bedroom door, who scurried ahead of them. He couldn't have been more than sixteen, but he had an air of confidence and self-assurance about him.

"This way, my lord," the lad said, pointing ahead through the crush of people at the riverfront.

Night had begun to fall, but that hadn't lessened the number of people going about their business, it merely changed the characters involved. Instead of tradesmen with their carts and honest dock workers unloading ships, the streets that lined the way down to St. Katherine's Dock were packed with raucous sailors in search of a good time and two-bit whores who looked more than happy to give it to them. Thaddeus could almost smell the gin and beer in the air as they passed pubs with their doors open, inviting all and sundry in for business.

"Is it much farther?" he asked the lad leading them, tension replacing the earlier elation he'd felt, especially when an inebriated sailor reached for Imogen, as though she were on the menu for the evening.

"It's right down at the end of one of the piers, my lord," the young man said, hurrying on.

"I do hope we get there quickly," Imogen said in a hushed voice. "I'm not sure I like this part of town at night."

"It's enjoyable if you're here for a bit of fun," Thaddeus said, pulling her closer to him as they picked up their pace. "But not so much for a lady as fine as you."

"Do you think I'm fine?" she asked, glancing hopefully up at him. "I mean, after all we've done." Her cheeks took on a rosy hue.

Thaddeus laughed. "I think you're the most beautiful and wonderful woman in all of Christendom."

He would have leaned in to kiss her, but another

sailor grabbed for her, clamping a hand around her upper arm. Only, as it turned out, it wasn't a sailor at all.

"I've got you at last," Lord Cunningham said, an infernal light in his eyes.

"You're not getting away this time." Lord Marlowe stood right behind him, looking as though he would strangle Thaddeus the way Thaddeus had almost strangled him.

Imogen shrieked and tried to pull away from Lord Cunningham. "Let go of me," she shouted, as strong as he'd ever heard her. Instead of cowering and bursting into tears, she looked as though she would fight Lord Cunningham until the bitter end.

Thaddeus wasn't about to leave the fighting to her. He didn't engage the men in a war of words or attempt an attack. First and foremost, they needed to get away. As fast and hard as he could, he swung the sack of Imogen's things around, slamming it down on Lord Cunningham's hand. The book fragment Imogen treasured so much must have hit Lord Cunningham's bone, because he cried out and let go of Imogen's arm. As soon as she was free, Thaddeus hoisted the sack over his shoulder again and yanked Imogen forward.

"Run," he hissed, closing his arm around her and whisking her away.

Running was easier said than done. The throng of people crowding around them didn't break ranks to let them through. Instead, they seemed far more interested in watching to see what was going on. Thaddeus had to shove men bigger than him aside and dart around painted women with their breasts falling out of their bodices to put any sort of distance at all between him and Imogen and Lord Cunningham and Lord Marlowe. At least the crowd held the two villains back as much as they impeded Thaddeus and Imogen's escape.

"In here," the young man, who was still leading them, called from the entrance to an alley several yards ahead.

Thaddeus tightened his grip on Imogen's hand and darted after the boy. He instantly worried he'd made the wrong decision when the narrow alley proved to be pitch black. At least they could move faster.

"I don't like this," Imogen said in a wary voice. She tugged against him slightly in resistance, as if attempting to go slower so she could feel her way.

"It's all right," the lad called. "I know this way. You won't trip over nothin'."

Thaddeus doubted the truth of that as his boot hit something foul and squishy, but he headed on, sweeping Imogen along with him. "I can see a light at the end," he told her.

That sped Imogen up a bit. That and her father's shout from the far end of the alley.

"Stop at once," Lord Marlowe called. "It's useless to keep going. We have agents working with us to catch you."

"I will wed and bed you yet, you bitch," Lord Cunningham added.

"No," Imogen shouted, pressing ahead and even outpacing Thaddeus for a moment. "You will not."

They burst out the other end of the alley. Thaddeus nearly sang in triumph when they found themselves right along the water's edge. The path they raced along to get to the pier was narrow and slippery as the tide lapped against the boards underneath, but anything that had the potential to slow them down or trip them up might also keep Lord Cunningham and Lord Marlowe at bay.

"The *Lucky Devil* is at the end of this pier," the young man shouted, scrambling on. His face glowed and he looked as though he was having far too much fun, but at least he was taking them where they needed to go.

The way would have been easier if not for a load of crates and barrels that practically formed mountains clogging the pier. Thaddeus was prepared to follow the lad's lead and leap over the first of them, clutching Imogen's sack tightly, before realizing that Imogen would never be able to manage that sort of feat.

"Here," he said, grasping her around the waist with the sack in one hand and hoisting her over a particularly large barrel. Once she was safe on the other side, he lunged over, and they continued on.

Seconds later, Lord Cunningham and Lord Marlowe reached the barrels.

"We've got you now," Lord Marlowe laughed. "My daughter is a weakling who can barely navigate the stairs, let alone this mess."

"I'm stronger than you think, Father," she growled, hiking her skirts and climbing over a small stack of crates.

Thaddeus had never been prouder of her, but they weren't free yet. Lord Marlowe growled like a rabid dog and leapt over every impediment that stood in his way. Lord Cunningham was slower, but it only took one of them to cause a major problem.

"There she is," the boy shouted from the clearing at the end of the unloaded cargo. "The *Lucky Devil*."

Thaddeus had never been so happy to see a ship in his life. He helped Imogen down from the last barrel and grasped her hand, dashing as fast as they were able toward the tall, proud ship. It looked like the sort of vessel that would sail around the world. It could take them to Scotland, but it might also carry them as far away as they needed to go to get away from Lord Marlowe and Lord Cunningham.

The trouble was that the gangplank leading up to the deck was guarded by half a dozen burly men, and they did not look the least bit inclined to let Thaddeus and Imogen dash aboard. Thaddeus could only pray that Rupert had paid their passage in full and given the men their names and descriptions.

Whatever the case, Thaddeus and Imogen were forced to skitter to a halt at the bottom of the gangplank. Imogen was panting and sweating, and though Thaddeus felt she had never looked more beautiful, he was desperate to get her onto the ship and away from her father.

"What do we have here?" the biggest of the men guarding the gangplank said with a salty grin. He had a Cornish accent, which only added to the eerie feeling that they were putting their lives in the hands of pirates.

"I'm Lord Thaddeus Herrington, and this is Lady Imogen, soon to be my wife," Thaddeus said, unable to fully catch his breath. "My brother, Lord Rupert Herrington, booked passage for us on this ship."

"Is that so?" the Cornishman said, glancing over his shoulder to his mates. They all chuckled, as though watching a drama on the stage instead of a desperate, real-life escape.

"Lord Herrington is to blame for this?" Lord Marlowe bellowed as he and Lord Cunningham raced up to the gangplank as well. "I'll have his hide."

"And I'll have this one's hide." Lord Cunningham reached for Imogen, his teeth bared in a snarl.

Thaddeus tugged Imogen out of his way, but he wasn't the only one who acted. All six of the ship guards rushed forward, crowding around Lord Cunningham and holding him back so fast that the blackguard's face went pale and he looked as though he were about to piss himself.

"We don't take well to assaulting women," the Cornishman said. "Not well at all."

Two of his mates drew long daggers from their belts. They looked as though they might flay Lord Cunningham alive. Lord Cunningham whimpered and cowered. Thaddeus would have enjoyed the sight, but he and Imogen were far from out of the woods.

"Please," he said, appealing to the Cornishman. "We need to board this ship as soon as possible."

"Do not let them board," Lord Marlowe countered. "This woman is my daughter. She is engaged to this man." He gestured to Lord Cunningham. "She is attempting to break her solemn vow and elope with this coward."

"I will not deny it," Imogen said, clinging to Thaddeus's arm. "I love him and I despise Lord Cunningham."

"I don't care whether you despise him or not, you will marry him," Lord Marlowe shouted.

"What seems to be the trouble here?"

The confrontation was interrupted as everyone glanced to the top of the gangplank. There stood a tall man with curling black hair, dressed in a coat as fine as any duke would have worn...twenty years prior. He had a rakish air to him and swaggered as he walked down the gangplank and into the fray.

His eyes went straight to Imogen and brightened. "Well, there's a siren if I ever saw one," he said in a husky voice.

Thaddeus bristled at the way he ogled Imogen's breasts, but he knew that both of their lives depended on the man. There was no doubt that he was Captain Devereux.

"This miscreant is attempting to run off with my fiancée," Lord Cunningham bellowed, jerking away from the sailors, who had backed off slightly at the appearance of their captain.

"And she is my daughter," Lord Marlowe added. "I will not allow her to run away."

Captain Devereux turned to Thaddeus, lifting his eyebrows slightly.

"She is the woman I love, sir," he said, slipping his arm around Imogen's waist and holding her closer. "I would die to get her away from these villains." He glared at Lord Marlowe and Lord Cunningham.

Captain Devereux glanced to each of them in turn, chuckling lightly. His grin widened. "Isn't this a fine situation," he said, then surprised Thaddeus by thumping him on the back. "Well done, sir. Your brother was right about your moxy."

Thaddeus nearly groaned in relief at the statement. So Rupert did know the man after all. Surely, he would help to sort out the entire situation and banish Lord Marlowe and Lord Cunningham, once and for all.

But Captain Devereux said, "We can't have young daughters and fiancées running off without so much as a by your leave." He shook his head at Imogen, the playful light still in his eyes. "That wouldn't be proper, my lady."

"But...but I love Thaddeus," Imogen pleaded with him. "And you cannot imagine the horrible things Lord Cunningham plans to do to me if I marry him."

Captain Devereux laughed. "Believe me, love, I can."

Imogen shrunk back, trembling slightly as she pressed herself against Thaddeus.

"I was given to understand you would help us, sir," Thaddeus said. "Not make the situation worse."

Captain Devereux shrugged. "And I will help you. I'll help you the way one man should help another." He paused, as if waiting for the chorus in a play to make a comment on the situation. When no one spoke, he went on with, "I'll give you and Lord What's His Name here —" he gestured to Lord Cunningham, "—a chance to solve this whole dispute as men should."

Lord Cunningham broke into a wicked smile. "Good. Swords it is, then."

"And don't wait for dawn," Lord Marlowe added. "I want this settled right here and now. Clear a space."

His order went completely unheeded by the delighted sailors watching the scene.

Captain Devereux laughed. "I don't mean that you should fight it out with swords," he said, snorting dismissively at Lord Cunningham.

"Pistols, then," Lord Cunningham said, standing straighter and sniffing.

"I don't have pistols or swords," Thaddeus said, more anxious than he wanted to admit. He'd been trained a bit with both, but by the look on Lord Cunningham's sour face, he was outmatched either way.

"I don't mean for you to duel at all," Captain Devereux said.

"Then what is your meaning, sir?" Lord Marlowe snapped.

Captain Devereux looked as though he was enjoying

the situation far too much. "I mean cards, of course," he said, bursting into a grin.

"Cards!" His men burst into shouts and cheers of approval.

"And it just so happens that I have everything set up on deck for a quick round of cards before we set sail," Captain Devereux finished.

"This is preposterous," Lord Cunningham barked. "Give me my fiancée at once."

"No!" Thaddeus and Imogen shouted at once. Thaddeus pulled Imogen toward the gangplank, convinced he could make a break for it. But once they made it aboard the ship, there was no guarantee Captain Devereux would let them stay there.

"Suit yourself," Captain Devereux said, turning and heading back to his ship.

"Wait," Thaddeus called after him. "I'll play cards. I'll play for the right to keep Imogen by my side. Whatever game you'd like."

"That's the spirit." Captain Devereux marched back to give him another slap on the back. "And you?" he asked Lord Cunningham and Lord Marlowe.

The two blackguards exchanged sullen looks. They didn't seem too keen on each other, let alone cards. If everything went wrong, Thaddeus was convinced he could use that to his advantage.

"All right," Lord Marlowe grumbled at last. "I'll agree to play cards for my daughter." He glanced to Lord Cunningham in question.

"I don't see that I have any choice," Lord Cunningham answered. "At least there will be two of us playing for the chit instead of one."

"Marvelous," Captain Devereux said, clapping his hands, then gesturing for everyone to follow him up the gangplank. "And if I win her, I'll show her what she's missing with the lot of you."

"If you win her?" Thaddeus asked, a few steps behind the man.

"Yes, of course," Captain Devereux said with a wink. "Consider it fare for passage. If I win."

"I'm not sure I like this idea," Imogen whispered as they made it to the ship's deck at last.

"I hate it," Thaddeus grumbled in reply. "But at the moment, we don't have any other choice."

CHAPTER 10

*I*mogen had never been aboard a ship in her life. She might have found the whole experience fascinating and rushed to explore the various decks, peer over the side into the dark water of the Thames, or even attempt to climb the rigging. But with her freedom at stake, all she wanted to do was stick as close to Thaddeus's side as possible.

"You weren't lying when you said you were already set up for a game," Lord Cunningham observed once he and Imogen's father were aboard. "Is this some sort of trick?"

"No, no, not at all," Captain Devereux laughed, slapping him hard on the back as he stepped over the railing onto the main deck. "As I said, we were playing before you got here."

That much seemed true enough. The round table in the center of the main deck was already scattered with cards and various coins. A few men who appeared to be officers of some sort got up from the table, taking sloppy mugs of beer with them. Night had fallen almost completely, but so many lanterns had been hung from the rigging and placed around the deck that it could have been a busy market in the middle of the afternoon. The whole thing had a vaguely magical quality to it.

"Come, gentlemen, come." Captain Devereux strode over to the table, gathering up the cards and taking a seat himself. "Let's get started. Time and tide wait for no man, particularly when there is a pretty girl involved."

Imogen moved with Thaddeus when he approached the table, doing her best to keep her distance from her father and Lord Cunningham. Neither of those two seemed excited about the game. Her father's face was pinched in pure annoyance.

"What right have you to play for my daughter?" her father asked, jerking back one of the chairs to take a seat. "You have no stake in this dispute."

"I have a stake in every dispute on my ship," Captain Devereux said, shuffling the cards. He twisted to call over his shoulder, "Mergen! Come be dealer, since I'm playing."

"Yes, captain," a short man with a large moustache and a genial smile darted forward, taking a seat at the table.

Thaddeus gave Imogen's hand a squeeze, his expression deadly serious, and handed her sack over before sitting at the chair beside the captain. Lord Cunningham grudgingly sat beside Imogen's father, muttering something to him that she couldn't make out.

What surprised Imogen, and everyone else, was that the young lad from the inn who had led them to the *Lucky Devil* slipped into the final open chair at the table.

"What is the meaning of this?" Lord Cunningham growled, attempting to stare down the young man and perhaps frighten him off.

His efforts had the opposite effect. The young man grinned back at him and declared, "I want to play too. I'm good at cards, I am. And I've been saving for just such an occasion."

He drew a small sack of coins from his waistcoat and upended it on the table. A meager amount of coins spilled into a pile. It wasn't much by the standards Imogen was used to, but she imagined it was quite a bit for a servant employed in a dockside inn.

"This is ridiculous," Imogen's father sniffed.

Captain Devereux obviously thought otherwise. "Good for you, lad," he laughed, punching him playfully in the arm. "What's your name, son?"

"Daniel," the young man said. "Daniel Long."

"Well then, Daniel Long, welcome to our game."

"But we're playing for possession of my daughter," Imogen's father growled. "What right does this boy have to her?"

"We're playing for money as well, aren't we?" Captain Devereux said, staring around the table at each player and daring them to contradict him. "Last man out wins the fair Lady Imogen's hand."

"I don't think that's fair," her father started.

Lord Cunningham stopped his complaint by gripping his arm. "How much money do you think that whelp has on him?" he said in a menacing voice. "Not as much as you or I, that much is certain."

Imogen's heart sank. He was right. Thaddeus didn't have much to his name, seeing as he was the younger son of an earl who was barely up to the mark.

He surprised them all by drawing a fairly large purse of coins from his jacket. "I still have the money Saif Khan gave me," he told Imogen, placing the purse on the table.

"But that's for our future," she whispered, dreading what would happen if he lost it and her. She hugged her sack of belongings, comforted somewhat by the hard edges of *The Secrets of Love* inside.

Her father and Lord Cunningham had produced their ready money, as did the captain, and the men set about arranging their coins in stacks and piles, anything that might make it appear as though they had more than was there.

"Vingt-et-un, I think," Captain Devereux said, nodding to Mr. Mergen, who sat, poised and ready to deal cards. "We'll keep it simple so we can get things over quickly."

"Agreed," Thaddeus said. He glanced over his shoulder to Imogen—who rather felt as though the boat were wobbling on the high seas already, seeing as so much was at stake—before turning to glare at her father and Lord Cunningham.

"Vingt-et-un," Daniel Long said with a slight frown. "That's the one where we're each dealt cards and we have to make twenty-one without going over, right?"

Thaddeus winced at the young man's ignorance. Imogen's father and Lord Cunningham exchanged chuckles. Captain Devereux even looked sorry for the lad. "That's the one," he said. "Mergen, the first round, if you please."

The initial cards were dealt and the men made their first bets. Imogen held her breath, beyond anxious over how the game might proceed. Thaddeus had to play against more than just her father and Lord Cunningham. Two strangers were also vying for her, though she didn't think young Mr. Long had a chance. Captain Devereux was a different kettle of fish, though. In all her panic and worry over running away with Thaddeus, she had never once considered that she might end up the prisoner of a third man entirely.

"What a shame," Captain Devereux said as Imogen's father slammed his cards on the table. "Twenty-six. Bad luck there."

Thaddeus won the hand, which came as an immense relief to Imogen. But he lost the next three. Her stomach twisted as the very real possibility of being lost forever loomed before her. The only saving grace was that no single man at the table seemed to gain the upper hand. Lord Cunningham won a hand, but then lost twice as much money as he'd won on the next. Captain Devereux played well and gained a small pile of coins, only to throw it all away on what Imogen considered careless betting on the next hand. His betting was so careless that she wondered if he were taking the game seriously. Mr. Long didn't win a single hand, but he bet wisely and only lost a pittance with each hand, whereas the others seemed to want to drive the stakes up as high as possible right from the start.

Her suspicion was confirmed when her father cursed under his breath and shoved the entirety of his money into the pot after being dealt two cards. "Enough of this," he growled. "We end this now."

"I'm out," Mr. Long said immediately, putting down his cards.

"Me too." Thaddeus followed suit, backing out of the hand.

Imogen's father was furious. "You can't do that. Play, you coward."

"He has every right to sit out if he doesn't think he has the cards," Captain Devereux said, maintaining a level head. "I, however, have the cards." He counted out an equivalent amount of coins to those her father had bet and shoved them into the middle.

"I'm in as well," Lord Cunningham said, an infernal light in his eyes. He pushed a pile of coins into the huge pot.

Imogen's father's gamble failed spectacularly. He only had nineteen, but Captain Devereux made twenty. But

Lord Cunningham ended up with twenty-one and took the pot. That knocked her father out of the game entirely, but every other player survived. It wasn't ideal, but it was one less chance that Imogen would end up being dragged off by Lord Cunningham at the end of the night.

Captain Devereux's fortunes were so badly depleted that he ended up out of the game on the very next hand. Imogen was more relieved than she thought she would be. "It's down to you three, now," he said, leaning back in his seat with a grin.

"Let's end this," Lord Cunningham said, staring at Thaddeus with a wolfish grin. "I want my bride in my bed, where she belongs, before sunrise."

Thaddeus drew in a long, anxious breath. He must have been thinking what Imogen was thinking, that he didn't have enough money left to mount a real challenge to Lord Cunningham. She gripped the back of his chair, glancing around for ways they still might be able to escape if and when Lord Cunningham won.

The next hand was dealt, but it didn't proceed at all the way Imogen expected it to. Lord Cunningham came out with an aggressive bet and Thaddeus matched it. But then Mr. Long shoved all his coins forward without a word.

"Are you sure you want to do that, boy?" Captain Devereux asked, his lips twitching into a grin.

"Yes, sir," Mr. Long said, staring intently, and somewhat confusedly, at his cards.

Lord Cunningham chuckled and matched the bet. Thaddeus matched it as well.

The final round of cards were dealt, and suddenly, Lord Cunningham's smug grin turned into a scowl. He muttered something and threw his cards on the table. That left Thaddeus and Mr. Long, and when all bets were matched and the cards turned over, Thaddeus had nineteen and Mr. Long twenty-one.

"Well played, son," Captain Devereux said, slapping Mr. Long's shoulder. "Good for you."

Mr. Long simply smiled, looking relieved. He had reason to look relieved as well. The massive pile of coins was now in front of him. It didn't take much for Imogen to see that he now held a far greater sum in front of him than any of the others.

"I'm out," Thaddeus said, his voice haunted.

Imogen blinked and pressed a hand to her stomach. "You're...out?"

He twisted to look up at her. His face had gone pale and his expression was miserable. "That was it. That was the last of Saif Khan's money."

"You lost it?" she asked, barely above a whisper.

"Deal the cards, Mergen," Captain Devereux ordered.

"Wait." Imogen tried to stop him. "You can't. There has to be another way. Can Thaddeus bet something else? Could he write a promissory note? Anything?"

"I always allow promissory notes and bets in kind at

my table," Captain Devereux said. "But it's a bit too late for that."

"Yes, it's a bit too late," Lord Cunningham said, adding a wicked laugh as he picked up the cards that had already been dealt to him.

"No," Imogen gasped. Thaddeus had gone out and the game was down to Lord Cunningham and Mr. Long. Her world was well and truly about to be tipped upside down.

As soon as the betting began, Lord Cunningham shoved all his money into the center of the table. "Beat that, boy," he growled at Mr. Long.

"All right," Mr. Long said. He pushed his entire pile into the table as well.

"Now deal," Lord Cunningham hissed at Mr. Mergen.

"Hold on there." Captain Devereux held up his hands. "The boy's bet a considerably larger sum of money than you. You have to match it."

"I'll write a note," Lord Cunningham growled. "Fetch me some paper."

Several of the sailors dashed off to do just that, but as they searched, Captain Devereux said, "That note will have to be for something comparable to the lovely Lady Imogen here."

"What?" Lord Cunningham snapped. "The difference in money cannot be more than a guinea or two."

"But Lady Imogen is worth more than a guinea or

two," the captain argued. "What else have you got to bet that matches her."

"I don't have to bet anything—"

"So you're saying you can't match the value of the prize?" Captain Devereux interrupted him.

"I didn't say—"

"I suppose that means you're out then," the captain went on, gesturing for Mergen—who had already started to deal—to take back Lord Cunningham's cards.

"Wait." Lord Cunningham slapped a hand over his cards, but didn't look as though he had a clue what to do next.

A thrill of hope passed through Imogen's heart. Perhaps the captain was on their side after all. Perhaps the whole game had been orchestrated to have the outcome she and Thaddeus wanted.

Her hopes were dashed when a sailor plunked a piece of paper and a pencil in front of Lord Cunningham and he grumbled, "All right, then. If you insist, I have a small property on Oxford Street. I purchased it as an investment, but it's done nothing for me. Would that suffice?"

"A property on Oxford Street?" Mr. Long's eyes lit up. He glanced to Captain Devereux, who shrugged and nodded, then back to Lord Cunningham. "Yes, that'll do quite nicely."

Lord Cunningham peeked at his cards, muttered under his breath, and rushed to write out a note, then tossed it in the center of the table with the rest of the coins.

"Are you mad, man?" Imogen's father asked him.

"The boy's a novice. He cannot possibly win." He leaned closer and said. "He doesn't have my cards."

"Well then," Captain Devereux said with a laugh. "This evening turned quite interesting. Deal on, Mergen."

"Aye, aye, captain," Mr. Mergen said, then dealt the last cards.

It was over in less than five seconds. As soon as Lord Cunningham and Mr. Long picked up their cards, Lord Cunningham turned a putrid shade of green and Mr. Long burst out in a laugh. Both threw their cards on the table—Lord Cunningham in disgust as he revealed an incredibly unlikely twenty-two, and Mr. Long in triumph as he revealed an equally long-shot twenty-one. The game was over. Mr. Long had won.

Imogen's life and fate were in the hands of a sixteen-year-old boy.

"Lucky Devil indeed," Captain Devereux laughed as Mr. Long snatched at the promissory note, tucking it away, then stood to scoop up his winnings.

"This is preposterous," Lord Cunningham boomed, rising and looking as though he would turn the table over. "I refuse to abide by this game. It was obviously fixed."

"You think a sixteen-year-old boy from an inn fixed a spur-of-the-moment card game?" Thaddeus asked, standing as well.

All of the men were on their feet in a trice. Lord Cunningham attempted to lunge toward Imogen, but the table stood between them, and within seconds, Thaddeus stood between them as well.

"Hand her over at once," Imogen's father shouted. "She is my daughter and I will say what becomes of her."

"You will not touch her," Thaddeus said. "She is the woman I love."

Lord Cunningham backed away from the table, only to leap at Thaddeus. Thaddeus balled his hands into fists, ready to fight. But Captain Devereux jumped between them, holding them apart.

"You agreed to the terms of the game, gentlemen," he said in a voice full of command. Imogen imagined that his men would follow him off the edge of the world with a voice and presence like that. "You agreed, and now you must abide by the terms."

"The game was nonsense, a farce," Imogen's father railed.

"I will not—" Lord Cunningham started.

"Men, what do we do with cheats who fail to abide by the rules of a game they agreed to play?" Captain Devereux asked.

That was all it took. With a victorious shout, half a dozen of the burly sailors rushed forward. They grabbed Lord Cunningham and Imogen's father and hoisted them into the air.

"Put me down, you cur!"

"Unhand me!"

Their cries went unheeded as the sailors carried them to the edge of the ship. Imogen and Thaddeus followed, Captain Devereux by their side.

"By your leave, captain?" one of the sailors asked.

"Carry on," Captain Devereux said with a wave of his hand.

Another cry rose from the men, and without any further ado, they tossed Lord Cunningham and Imogen's father over the side of the ship and into the Thames. Twin splashes told Imogen they were well and truly gone. She wasn't sure she even cared if they drowned or if they managed to swim to the nearest dock and crawl ashore.

She turned to Thaddeus. "They're gone," she said, breathless and brimming with hope that seemed as though it might actually take hold for a change.

"They are," Thaddeus said, reaching for her. "And now we can be together."

"Hold on there." Captain Devereux stepped between them prying them apart with a delighted grin. "You can't go handling Mr. Long's property like that. Mr. Long?" he called over his shoulder to the table.

Mr. Long was still shoving coins into the sack he'd brought with him, his pockets, his hat, and anything that would hold them. He glanced up with a curious look when his name was called.

"Mr. Long," Captain Devereux said, touching Imogen's arm lightly and escorting her back to the table,

Thaddeus behind them. "This man would like to make off with your property."

"Hmm?" Mr. Long blinked. His young face was pink with delight and his blue eyes glittered. "Oh. Her. It's all right, you can have her," he told Thaddeus. "She's a bit too la-dee-da for me anyhow."

Imogen laughed in spite of herself. "Thank you, Mr. Long." She broke away from Captain Devereux and planted a kiss on his cheek.

"Don't make him second-guess his generosity," Thaddeus said with a laugh of his own. He stepped forward to shake Mr. Long's hand. "I am eternally grateful, Mr. Long, and whatever help I can give you in the future is yours."

"Thank you, my lord." Mr. Long pumped his hand vigorously. "A property on Oxford Street. Can you imagine? And here I am, a boy from Limehouse, barely out of short pants."

"What are you going to do with the property?" Imogen asked.

Mr. Long tilted his head to the side for a moment, then said, "I think I'll make it a pub."

"Good for you, lad." Captain Devereux stepped forward to shake his hand as well. When he had the young man in a tight grip, he asked, "You counted the cards, didn't you?"

"Every last one of them, sir," Mr. Long confessed.

Imogen blew out a breath and laughed all over again. So young Daniel Long had been playing them all the entire time. He had far more experience with cards than he'd let on, that much was certain. Which meant that her father and Lord Cunningham hadn't stood a chance from the start. Neither had Thaddeus, for that matter, but at least the young man wasn't the sort to part lovers.

"Oh, and I guess this can be a wedding present," Mr. Long said, handing one of the sacks of coins he'd filled to Thaddeus. "Get you off on the right start and all," he added.

"You don't have to," Thaddeus said, taking the sack all the same.

"I want to," Mr. Long said. He then touched his free hand to his forehead and started toward the gangplank. "Cheers. I must get this lot taken care of before the real thieves and cutpurses come out for the night."

As soon as he was gone, Thaddeus let out a breath of relief and turned to hold his arms out to Imogen. She rushed into them, hugging him for all she was worth and kissing him for good measure. Behind him, Captain Devereux gave the orders for his crew to lift anchor and set out.

"At last," Imogen said, sliding her arms around Thaddeus's neck and smiling at him, her heart filled with joy. "At last, those evil men are behind us and we can start our life together."

"And a beautiful life it will be," Thaddeus finished, sealing his words with a kiss.

EPILOGUE

*S*cotland in January was chilly, bleak, and more than a little damp, but Imogen had never been happier. Even though the tiny cottage she and Thaddeus had rented by the sea came with a few extra tenants that they hadn't expected.

"Catch him, catch him," Imogen laughed and squealed as Thaddeus charged through the small front room with a broom, attempting to whisk the starling that had built a nest in the rafters out one of the windows.

"I'm trying to," Thaddeus laughed along with her. "The blighter keeps giving me the slip."

The terrified bird twittered and swooped, darting every which way in the small room except toward the window. Imogen shrieked with giggles as it dove toward her hair, which she'd left undone, in spite of the scandal of wearing it that way during the day.

Thaddeus chased the bird closer to the window only

to trip over the edge of the faded, braided rug in the center of the room. With a surprised whoop, he tumbled forward, landing, sprawled, on the threadbare sofa that faced the fireplace. Imogen laughed so hard she had to grip her sides as the starling flew back to its lofty nest. She collapsed onto the sofa with Thaddeus, letting out a long, happy sigh.

"I think we will have to live with him," she said, still giggling.

Thaddeus righted himself. He tossed the broom aside, then slipped his arm around Imogen's shoulders. "I think you're right there. But I cannot be responsible for the things he might see."

He leaned toward her, closing his mouth over hers and a hand over her breast. Imogen's giggles turned into a deep sigh as she surged into his embrace. In the months that had passed since they'd escaped from London and made a new life for themselves in Scotland as man and wife, she'd grown bold when it came to expressing her desire for him. She slid her tongue against his, reaching for the front of his breeches. When she found him already half hard and growing fast, she hummed deep in her throat.

"I don't care one bit that we don't have a penny to our name," she moaned, caressing and encouraging him. "This is worth far more than money."

"We have some money," he reminded her, though money seemed to be the least of his concerns.

He tipped her back against the arm of the sofa and

sought out her legs under the hem of her skirt. With a quick movement and sin sparkling in his eyes, he lifted one of her legs up over the back of the chair, then proceeded to disappear beneath her skirts.

Imogen tilted her head back and let out a pleasure sigh as his mouth made contact with her sex. He'd pleasured her a hundred times and more since their marriage, but she never grew tired of the heady sensation of arousal. Her body was instantly alive with arousal, and she let out another cry.

At least, until there was a knock at the door. "Mrs. Herrington? Oh, Mrs. Herrington. I was just down at the post office and as there was a letter for you, I thought I would just take it with me and—oh!" Their elderly neighbor, Mrs. Tucker, gasped as she let herself into the cottage and found Imogen spread out in a position of decadence. "Oh, my! Oh, I never...."

Thaddeus darted out from under Imogen's skirts, face red and lips shining with moisture. He quickly rubbed them with the sleeve of his shirt and stood as Imogen yelped and threw herself off the sofa. She landed on her knees—which were already a bit sore from other wicked activities she and Thaddeus had engaged in earlier in the day—before snapping straight and standing as best she could.

"You have a letter for me, Mrs. Tucker?" she asked in a squeaky voice.

"I do." Mrs. Tucker handed the letter over in a hurry, red as a beet and stammering in her attempt to form another sentence. "Oh, my. Oh, dear. I didn't intend to interrupt you newlyweds. I was young once myself and... oh dear!"

The poor old woman dashed for the door, running out of the house. Of all things, the starling swooped down and flew after her through the open door.

Once they were both gone, Thaddeus broke into laughter as he crossed to shut—and lock—the door, and Imogen glanced at the letter.

"It's from Alice," she gasped, brimming with excitement. "And it's been posted from Aegiria."

"Aegiria?" Thaddeus asked. "Isn't that the tiny Scandinavian island where Count Fabian Camoni is from?"

"It is." Imogen's heart filled with worry as she tore open the envelope. "That can only mean that Father has married Alice off to the man after all."

"I always liked Count Camoni," Thaddeus said with a slight frown as he came to read over Imogen's shoulder.

"*Dear Imogen and Thaddeus,*" Imogen read aloud. "*As I am certain you will know by the Aegirian post mark on this letter, I have married Count Camoni after all, as Father wished.*" Imogen glanced to Thaddeus. "Oh, dear. I hope she's not too disappointed."

Thaddeus's brow went up as he read the rest of the letter. "Read on. It's not as bad as you think."

Imogen turned back to the letter. "*As it turns out, Fabian is not quite the villain I thought he was. Though it took me long enough to come to that conclusion. Our*

Christmas wedding was both a trial, thanks to Father, and a revelation. But it almost didn't take place. I...."

Imogen stopped reading and let out a breath on a sigh as Thaddeus stepped flush against her, bending to nibble at her neck. He reached around to cup her breasts as well, kneading at first, then scooping his hand beneath her neckline to tease her nipple.

"How can I possibly read a letter from my sister with you tormenting me so?" Imogen asked, a laugh low in her throat.

"There will be time to read letters later," Thaddeus said, plucking the paper from her and tossing it aside. With that done, he lifted her off her feet and spread her across the sofa once more. "Now, where were we?" he asked before disappearing under her skirts once more.

Imogen let out a cry as his mouth closed over her. She loved her sister dearly, but if there was one thing *The Secrets of Love* had taught her, it was that a woman needed to be bold in the pursuit of pleasure. Whatever Alice had to say, she would learn later. At the moment, she had a husband to love and be loved by.

I HOPE YOU HAVE ENJOYED IMOGEN AND THADDEUS'S story! So all's well that ends well for at least one of the Marlowe girls. But what about Alice and Lettuce? Are you curious about Alice and Fabian's Christmas wedding? You can find out all about it now in *The*

Holiday Hussy, my contribution to the *Once Upon a Christmas Wedding* box set!

And don't worry, Lettuce's story, *The Captive Vixen*, is coming in early January as part of the *Once Upon a Pirate* box set. Which means, yes, a sexy pirate is indeed involved!

IF YOU ENJOYED THIS BOOK AND WOULD LIKE TO HEAR more from me, please sign up for my newsletter! When you sign up, you'll get a free, full-length novella, *A Passionate Deception*. Victorian identity theft has never been so exciting in this story of hope, tricks, and starting over. Part of my *West Meets East* series, *A Passionate Deception* can be read as a stand-alone. Pick up your free copy today by signing up to receive my newsletter (which I only send out when I have a new release)!

SIGN UP HERE: HTTP://EEPURL.COM/CBAVMH

Click here for a complete list of other works by Merry Farmer.

ABOUT THE AUTHOR

I hope you have enjoyed *The Faithful Siren*. If you'd like to be the first to learn about when new books in the series come out and more, please sign up for my newsletter here: http://eepurl.com/cbaVMH And remember, Read it, Review it, Share it! For a complete list of works by Merry Farmer with links, please visit http://wp.me/P5ttjb-14F.

Merry Farmer is an award-winning novelist who lives in suburban Philadelphia with her cats, Torpedo, her grumpy old man, and Justine, her hyperactive new baby. She has been writing since she was ten years old and realized one day that she didn't have to wait for the teacher to assign a creative writing project to write something. It was the best day of her life. She then went on to earn not one but two degrees in History so that she would always have something to write about. Her books have reached the Top 100 at Amazon, iBooks, and Barnes & Noble, and have been named finalists in the prestigious RONE and Rom Com Reader's Crown awards.

ACKNOWLEDGMENTS

I owe a huge debt of gratitude to my awesome beta-readers, Caroline Lee and Jolene Stewart, for their suggestions and advice. And double thanks to Julie Tague, for being a truly excellent editor and assistant! Thanks also to the members of the Historical Harlots Facebook Group, who provide me with all sorts of inspiration!

Click here for a complete list of other works by Merry Farmer.

Made in the USA
Las Vegas, NV
01 November 2021

33499273R10085